D0991198

# LOVES, LIES AND MARRIAGE

## 1821

Teresa knows that had she been a boy her father, Sir Hubert Bryan would have taken her into his Shipping Company. So, when she finally leaves school that is what she tells him she wishes to do.

Sir Hubert has become very rich, and is therefore able to help his friend the Marquess of Walstoke, who had been so hard up that he was forced to sell many of the treasures from his home – Stoke Palace.

The two men make it their hobby to restore the Palace to its former glory.

Having no son, the Marquess makes his nephew Edward, the Earl of Lanbourne, who is always known as Harry, his heir. When they learn that Harry is planning to marry an actress, the two men work out a plan to prevent him from ruining his life.

How they plan a mock marriage, with Sir Hubert's daughter Teresa, and how the "Bridle Couple" on their way to Bourne Hall, Harry's Elizabethan house, run into danger, and how Teresa nurses Harry and makes the house as beautiful as it was when his mother was alive are all told in this exciting 514th book by Barbara Cartland.

# LOVE, LIES AND MARRIAGE

by

Barbara Cartland

SEVERN HOUSE PUBLISHERS

This first world edition published in Great Britain 1992 by
SEVERN HOUSE PUBLISHERS LTD of
35 Manor Road, Wallington, Surrey SM6 0BW
First published in the U.S.A. 1992 by
SEVERN HOUSE PUBLISHERS INC of
475 Fifth Avenue, New York, NY 10017–6220



British Library Cataloguing in Publication Data
Cartland, Barbara
Love, Lies and Marriage
I. Title
823.912 [F]

ISBN 0-7278-4415-6

Typeset in Linotron Sabon by
Hewer Text Composition Services, Edinburgh
Printed and bound in Great Britain by
Dotesios Limited, Trowbridge, Wiltshire

## AUTHOR'S NOTE

Elizabeth Farren, who was to become one of England's best loved actresses, was born in 1759. Her father was a jovial drunk who had been an apothecary in Cork. He joined a troupe of players who toured Ireland, and ended up in Liverpool where he met and married a barmaid.

They had two daughters, Margaret and Elizabeth – a fair-haired child with blue eyes who played boy roles in Shakespeare.

She was introduced to the London stage when she was a tall, willowy girl who was not particularly beautiful, but who had a very expressive face. Elizabeth appeared at Drury Lane in 1778, and her *métier* was unquestionably Comedy.

She was very virtuous but among the many men who vainly sought her favours, Elizabeth liked the Earl of Derby the best. At an entertainment given by the Duke of Richmond, the Earl told Elizabeth he was deeply in love with her.

Unfortunately he had a wife, a confirmed invalid whom he seldom saw, but she was a barrier that stood between them. So the Earl accepted that only by marriage could he possess Elizabeth, but it was impossible for him to leave his wife.

Instead he and Elizabeth agreed to an intimate, but platonic friendship. They became lovers without giving themselves to each other. Despite this strange relationship their love never changed and they continued in this manner for twenty years.

Then in March, 1797, the Earl's wife died and he was at last free to marry his adorable, virtuous Elizabeth. They at once started to make arrangements for their wedding which took place by special licence on May 1st of that year. On April 7th, 1797, Elizabeth made her last stage appearance playing Lady Teazle in *The School for Scandal*.

As everybody knew the story of Elizabeth and the Earl with their idealised romance and devotion to each other, the theatre was packed.

Elizabeth was thirty-eight when she became the Countess of Derby and they spent their honeymoon at Epsom. But it only lasted for two days because Elizabeth was anxious to be presented at Court. She was the first Peeress who had ever been an actress and when she appeared before the Queen she had an overwhelming desire to talk.

She told Her Majesty that it was one of the most blissful moments of her life to appear before her in a new "character part".

The Queen was not amused and replied: "Cannot Your Ladyship forget her breeding?"

Feeling rebuffed, the new Countess, from that moment, never spoke of her connections with the theatre again.

She was however blissfully happy with her husband

and presented him with three children; one son and two daughters. They lived a life of perfect happiness with not a cloud in the sky. Elizabeth died at the age of seventy in 1829 at Knowsley, the county seat of the Earls of Derby. Her husband followed her five years later.

# ABOUT THE AUTHOR

Barbara Cartland, the world's most famous romantic novelist, who is also an historian, playwright, lecturer, political speaker and television personality, has now written over 517 books and sold over 500 million copies all over the world.

She has also had many historical works published and has written four autobiographies as well as the biographies of her mother and that of her brother, Ronald Cartland, who was the first Member of Parliament to be killed in the last war. This book has a preface by Sir Winston Churchill and has just been published with an introduction by the late Sir Arthur Bryant.

*Love at the Helm* a novel written with the help and inspiration of the late Earl Mountbatten of Burma, Great Uncle of His Royal Highness The Prince of Wales, is being sold for the Mountbatten Memorial Trust.

She has broken the world record for the last fourteen years by writing an average of twenty-three books a year. In the Guiness Book of Records she is listed as the world's top-selling author.

Miss Cartland in 1978 sang an Album of Love Songs with the Royal Philharmonic orchestra.

In private life Barbara Cartland, who is a Dame of Grace of the Order of St. John of Jerusalem, Chairman of the St. John Council in Hertfordshire and Deputy President of the St. John Ambulance Brigade, has fought for better conditions and salaries for Midwives and Nurses.

She championed the cause for the Elderly in 1956 instigating a Government Enquiry into the "Housing Conditions of Old People".

In 1962 she had the Law of England changed so that Local Authorities had to provide camps for their own Gypsies. This has meant that since then thousands and thousands of Gypsy children have been able to go to Sshool which they had never been able to do in the past, as their caravans were moved every twenty-four hours by the Police.

There are now fourteen camps in Hertfordshire and Barbara Cartland has her own Romany Gypsy Camp called Barbaraville by the Gypsies.

Her designs "Decorating with Love" are being sold all over the U.S.A. and the National Home Fashions League made her in 1981, "Woman of Achievement".

Barbara Cartland's book *Getting Older, Growing Younger* has been published in Great Britain and the U.S.A. and her fifth Cookery Book, *The Romance of Food* is now being used by the House of Commons.

In 1984 she received at Kennedy Airport, America's Bishop Wright Air Industry Award for her contribution to the development of aviation. In 1931 she and two R.A.F. Officers thought of, and carried, the first aeroplane-towed glider air-mail.

During the War she was Chief Lady Welfare Officer in Bedfordshire looking after 20,000 Service men and women. She thought of having a pool of Wedding Dresses at the War Office so a Service Bride could hire a gown for the day.

She bought 1,000 secondhand gowns without coupons for the A.T.S., the W.A.A.F.s and the W.R.E.N.S. In 1945 Barbara Cartland received the Certificate of Merit from Eastern Command.

In 1964 Barbara Cartland founded the National Association for Health of which she is the President, as a front for all the Health Stores and for any product made as alternative medicine.

This has now a £500,000,000 turnover a year, with one third going in export.

In January 1988 she received "La Medaille de Vermeil de la Ville de Paris", (the Gold Medal of Paris). This is the highest award to be given by the City of Paris for ACHIEVEMENT – 25 million books sold in France.

In March 1988 Barbara Cartland was asked by the Indian Government to open their Health Resort outside Delhi. This is almost the largest Health Resort in the world.

Barbara Cartland was received with great enthusiasm by her fans, who also fêted her at a Reception in the city and she received the gift of an embossed plate from the Government.

## OTHER BOOKS BY BARBARA CARTLAND

Other novels, over 500, the most recently published being:

Love in Ruins
A Coronation of Love
A Duel of Jewels
The Wicked Widow
The Duke is Trapped
Just a Wonderful Dream
Love and Cheetah
Drena and the Duke
A Dog, a Horse and a Heart
Never Lose Love
Spirit of Love
The Eyes of Love
The Duke's Dilemma
Saved by a Saint
Safe in Paradise
Beyond the Stars
The Innocent Imposter
The Incomparable
The Dare-Devil Duke
The Royal Rebuke
Love Runs In
Love Light of the Gods
The Dream and the Glory (In aid of the St. John Ambulance Brigade)

*Autobiographical and Biographical*:

The Isthmus Years 1919–1939
The Years of Opportunity 1939–1945
I Search for Rainbows 1945–1976
We Danced All Night 1919–1929
Ronald Cartland (With a foreword by Sir Winston Churchill)
Polly – My Wonderful Mother
I Seek the Miraculous

*Historical*:

Bewitching Women
The Outrageous Queen (The Story of Queen Christina of Sweden)
The Scandalous Life of King Carol
The Private Life of Charles II
The Private Life of Elizabeth, Empress of Austria
Josephine, Empress of France
Diane de Poitiers
Metternich – The Passionate Diplomat
A Year of Royal Days
Royal Jewels
Royal Eccentrics
Royal Lovers

*Sociology*:

You in the Home
The Fascinating Forties
Marriage for Moderns
Be Vivid, Be Vital
Love, Life and Sex
Vitamins for Vitality
Husbands and Wives
Men are Wonderful
Etiquette
The Many Facets of Love
Sex and the Teenager
The Book of Charm
Living Together
The Youth Secret
The Magic of Honey
The Book of Beauty and Health
Keep Young and Beautiful by Barbara Cartland and Elinor Glyn
Etiquette for Love and Romance
Barbara Cartland's Book of Health

*Cookery*:

Barbara Cartland's Health Food Cookery Book
Food for Love
Magic of Honey Cookbook
Recipes for Lovers
The Romance of Food

*Editor of*:

"The Common Problem" by Ronald Cartland (with a preface by the Rt. Hon. the Earl of Selborne, P.C.)
Barbara Cartland's Library of Love
Barbara Cartland's Library of Ancient Wisdom
"Written with Love". Passionate love letters selected by Barbara Cartland

*Drama*:

Blood Money
French Dressing

*Philosophy*:

Touch the Stars

*Radio Operetta*:

The Rose and the Violet (Music by Mark Lubbock) Performed in 1942.

*Radio Plays*:

The Caged Bird: An episode in the life of Elizabeth Empress of Austria. Performed in 1957.

*General*:

Barbara Cartland's Book of Useless Information with a Foreword by the Earl Mountbatten of Burma.
(In aid of the United World Colleges)
Love and Lovers (Picture Book)
The Light of Love (Prayer Book)
Barbara Cartland's Scrapbook
(In aid of the Royal Photographic Museum)
Romantic Royal Marriages
Barbara Cartland's Book of Celebrities
Getting Older, Growing Younger

*Verse*:

Lines on Life and Love

*Music*:

An Album of Love Songs sung with the Royal Philharmonic Orchestra.

*Films*:

A Hazard of Hearts
The Lady and the Highwayman
A Ghost in Monte Carlo

*Cartoons*:

Barbara Cartland Romances (Book of Cartoons) has recently been published in the U.S.A., Great Britain, and other parts of the world.

*Children*:

A Children's Pop-Up Book: "Princess to the Rescue"

*Videos*:

A Hazard of Hearts
The Lady and The Highwayman
A Ghost in Monte Carlo

# CHAPTER ONE

## *1821*

The Marquess of Walstoke walked into the Board-room. It was eleven o'clock and Sir Hubert Bryan, who was sitting at the top of the Conference Table, said, "You are very late!"

"I know," the Marquess answered, "but I did not leave the Duchess's party until two o'clock this morning."

"Was it a good party?" Sir Hubert asked.

"Very good!" the Marquess replied. He walked down the table to sit in his usual place.

A handsome man of nearly sixty, he carried himself with a pride and a dignity that made it obvious to everybody who met him that he was an aristocrat.

He was in fact extremely proud of his heritage, but he had, about ten years ago, been in deep water, though it was not entirely his fault. The war with

Napoleon had made a great number of Landowners poverty-stricken, for it was impossible, with so many men away fighting in Portugal and Spain, for the repairs needed on their Estates to be dealt with. Farmhouses had leaking roofs and the hedges of any estate grew wild and unwieldy.

It was then the Marquess had been fortunate enough to become friends with Sir Hubert Bryan, who was one of the outstanding businessmen in the country. He had started life in Liverpool, where he became an assistant to one of the biggest Shipowners.

Hubert Bryan, or as his enemies called him, Hue Brien, worked and fought his way to the top. When he was twenty-five, he was an extremely rich young man, and had a commanding personality which impressed all those who met him.

Quite by chance, he met the daughter of the Duke of Dorset at a luncheon given by the Corporation of Liverpool at which she and the Duke were the Guests of Honour. For the first time in his life, Hubert Bryan fell in love.

In ordinary circumstances he would have been swept aside by the Duke as someone of no importance whom he had no wish to know. But the Duke was, in fact, looking for some way by which he could increase his gradually diminishing finances. He thought perhaps shipping might help him where other investments had failed, so he invited Hubert Bryan to his country house which was about ten miles outside Liverpool.

That was the beginning of their association.

## 3

The Duke intended it to be an entirely business one, and so when the Liverpool Shipowner, whom he thought he was patronising, wanted to marry his daughter he was shocked, horrified and indignant. He actually forbade the two young people ever to see each other again.

Lady Elizabeth however paid no attention. She and Hubert Bryan (he had embellished his name by that time) met each other secretly.

The Duke discovered what was happening – there were always people ready to carry bad news. He flew into a rage, threatening and abusing Hubert Bryan. Then quite quietly the young man told him what he was worth.

The Duke was completely astounded. He had no idea that anyone so young could possibly have such a huge fortune, and made it himself.

Hubert Bryan also told him what he intended to do in the future.

The way he spoke was so impressive that, despite himself, the Duke believed him. It all ended quite simply with the Duke giving his consent to their marriage.

The years passed and he basked in the sunshine of his son-in-law's fortune. He forgot he had ever been so stupid as to oppose the marriage when he was first confronted with it. What was more, no one doubted that Lady Elizabeth was blissfully happy, but their only regret was that having had one child she could not have any more.

The Duke's granddaughter Teresa was a beauty

from the moment she was born. It was not surprising, as her father was an extremely handsome man, and her mother outstandingly beautiful. The Duke at one time had been certain his daughter would at least marry a Royal Prince.

It had a great deal to do with the Duke that Hubert Bryan was eventually Knighted. He had contributed to the importance of Liverpool, being extremely generous when he was asked to help the City financially, and it certainly pleased the Duke that his son-in-law had a title. Also that his income seemed to double and triple, year by year.

When Sir Hubert lost his wife it was a blow which would have destroyed a weaker man. He had never looked at another woman. When they had been married for sixteen years, they still behaved like sweethearts.

Because the pain of losing her was intolerable, Hubert merely worked harder than he ever had done before. His fleet of ships continued to grow in number, just as his money increased in the same way. The Duke died, but his place in Hubert Bryan's life was taken over by another aristocrat.

He had met the Marquess of Walstoke with his father-in-law, and he had been impressed by the example he gave the world of how an aristocrat should look, and how he should behave.

His manners were impeccable. He was as polite to a crossing-sweeper as he was to a Prince. No one had ever heard anyone say anything derogatory against the Marquess.

At the same time, the war had played havoc with his

finances. He was struggling ineffectually to keep Stoke Palace, which had been in his family for generations, from tumbling to the ground.

He had had to dismiss a great number of his servants, and those who worked for him on his Estate. To pension many of them he decided to sell one of his best pictures. Also the silver which had been in his family since the reign of Queen Anne.

And it was this silver which had brought him in contact with Sir Hubert Bryan.

Because, before the Auction, it was extolled in the newspapers, Sir Hubert thought it would be an addition to his own belongings. It was also in fact something he needed, for his wife had taught him to appreciate antiques. She had encouraged him to buy a fine house on a five-thousand acre estate, and had decorated it in the perfect taste she had inherited from her father.

She persuaded her husband to purchase pictures painted by the great Masters, and she had also begged him to collect fine china and other objects for the house, which was something with which previously he had never come in contact.

Because he loved his wife, and also because he had an extremely astute brain, he soon understood the value and prestige of having good taste.

Lady Elizabeth and Sir Hubert visited Auctions. Sometimes they were in private houses, at other times in Christie's Sale Rooms which had recently opened in London. When he brought her back something she appreciated, it gave him a thrill he had not known before.

Although Elizabeth was now dead, he continued to improve his house in the country, and also the one he had bought in London for Teresa. He thought when she finally left school her background must be a perfect frame for her beauty.

He realised that the Marquess of Walstoke's house was within driving distance of Liverpool, and he therefore called on him before the Auction asking if it was possible to see the silver that was to be put up for sale.

He arrived in a very luxurious carriage and had a commanding appearance. The servants, therefore, instead of directing him to the hall where the objects for sale had been laid out, showed him into the library, where the Marquess was sitting by the fireplace reading a book.

To say that Sir Hubert was impressed by the Marquess was to put it mildly. He realised that here was a man who he would like to emulate. He was also as precious and unique as any of the objects he intended to sell.

On the other hand, the Marquess liked Sir Hubert and talked to him as if he was his equal. He had of course heard about him and admired the brilliant way by which he had climbed to the top. The way he had assisted Liverpool, and his enormous possessions were known all over the country.

The two Gentlemen talked together for nearly two hours. When Sir Hubert left they were both aware that in some strange manner a new step forward had been taken in both their lives. The Auction was cancelled, and Hubert Bryan bought everything that was for sale, but kept the silver for himself and gave everything else back to the Marquess.

"It belongs here," he said looking round Stoke Palace, "and you cannot deprive whoever inherits this magnificent house of its treasures. You must make it as perfect as it must have been when it was first built."

The Marquess was deeply touched, but he was intelligent enough to know that Sir Hubert Bryan was not speaking out of charity. It was his way of creating something for posterity, and it did in fact give Sir Hubert a new interest besides increasing his fortune.

He tried to find out where the pictures the Marquess had previously sold had gone, and bought them back. There was some carved and gilded furniture from the reign of Charles II, but it took them both six months to discover their whereabouts before finally they ran them to earth.

They brought it back in triumph to Stoke Palace.

It delighted Sir Hubert as much as the Marquess to see the house, like a rose, coming into bloom. Everything was coming back where it had originally stood.

Sir Hubert met the Marquess's heir, who was not his son, but his nephew. The Marquess's only sister had married the Earl of Lanbourne, and lived in the South. He often saw her when he went down to London, and it was a terrible blow when both she and her husband were killed in a carriage accident.

They had one child, named Edward, but who was always called Harry. The Marquess had realised that the boy, who was then only seventeen, must make his home with him, both in Liverpool and in London.

When he told Sir Hubert about this, the latter said, "Well, all I can say is that he is a very lucky young man! Stoke Palace is already spoken of as one of the beauties of the County and by the time we have finished with it, it will not have its equal in any part of England."

The Marquess had laughed. "I only hope Harry appreciates the trouble we have taken for him."

"I am sure he will," Sir Hubert replied, "just as Teresa is thrilled, like her mother, with anything new with which I embellish her home."

He paused before he went on, "That reminds me – I want your opinion about a picture which I think should go over the mantelpiece in the Drawing Room at Berkeley Square."

"Have you found what we considered was needed there?" the Marquess asked.

"I think so," Sir Hubert replied. "At the same time I always, as you know, bow to your judgement where pictures are concerned."

The Marquess smiled. He was always delighted when his friend paid him the compliment of thinking his judgement was better than his own. The more he knew Sir Hubert, the more he realised how brilliantly clever he was in everything he undertook.

It was not just a question of money. His brain was, the Marquess thought, the equivalent, if not superior to, most of those Statesmen in the Government.

He also copied the Marquess in many of the distinctive ways which had made him an outstanding Gentlemen, in the proper meaning of the word.

Now the Marquess said "We will go and look at the picture this afternoon. I suppose we are having a meeting this morning?"

"We are," Sir Hubert replied. "The others will be arriving in about half-an-hour, but I wanted to see you alone."

The Marquess looked at him enquiringly. "I am rather late," he said, "but nevertheless, I am here."

To his surprise he realised that his friend Sir Hubert was feeling for words. It was unlike him, and he wondered what could be amiss. He was just about to ask if there had been a catastrophe in Liverpool, or alternatively, if one of the ships in which he too was now interested had been sunk at sea, when Sir Hubert said:

"I wanted to talk to you about Harry."

"About Harry?" the Marquess exclaimed in surprise.

Harry had come back from the war, where he had served under Wellington at the Battle of Waterloo.

He was only twenty when he joined the great Commander in France. When after Waterloo the war was over Harry stayed on in the Army of Occupation, and was there for nearly two years. On returning to London he began to enjoy all the things he had missed, for he had enlisted in the Army instead of going up to Oxford like so many of his friends.

He was exceedingly handsome and very well off, thanks to the money he had inherited from his father and the very generous allowance the Marquess gave him. He was therefore on the Invitation List of every important hostess, who considered him, as the Marquess knew only too well, a good matrimonial catch for their débutante daughters.

It was however characteristic of Harry to spend his time in other directions.

This was with married women, who were charming, exotic, and discreetly unfaithful to their husbands. Or inevitably with the irresistible "Cyprians" with which London abounded.

"The boy has to 'sow his wild oats'," the Marquess said often enough to Sir Hubert when he was presented with very large bills.

He also laughed when he was told of some of the pranks that Harry had played with the younger members of White's Club.

The Dowager Duchesses might look down their noses but the Marquess understood.

What pleased him was that Harry was extremely athletic, an excellent horseman, and invariably the winner of any Steeple chase or point-to-point he entered.

It delighted him that, thanks to Sir Hubert, he could afford the very best horses in his stables at Stoke Palace.

The same applied to the Mews, which had been

enlarged, behind the house he also had in Berkeley Square.

The Marquess had sold the house when he was in desperate straits before he met Sir Hubert. Sir Hubert had insisted he should buy it back, and once again it was known as "Walstoke House", as it had been in the past.

Harry lived there and always appeared delighted to see his Uncle when he came down from the North.

The Marquess had arrived three days ago. Both on the night he arrived, and the next, Harry had apologised for having a previous engagement he could not break.

"You go and enjoy yourself, my boy," the Marquess said. "It is what I did at your age, and something I have never regretted."

"I knew you would understand, Uncle Maurice," Harry said, "but I have a lot to talk about to you when we have the time."

"I am entirely at your disposal," the Marquess said grandly.

Harry had smiled at him before he had gone off in a closed carriage leaving the Marquess to dine alone. He wished then that he had arranged to dine with Sir Hubert on the other side of the Square. But as his dinner was waiting and he did not wish to disappoint the Chef, he had eaten alone.

Last night it was he who had an engagement with the Duchess of Devonshire. He was leaving the house when Harry came back to change. "Are you going out, Uncle Maurice?" he asked.

"I am afraid so," the Marquess replied.

"I was hoping we could have dinner together," Harry said, "but never mind. I do not suppose you are in a hurry to leave London?"

"As I said before, I am at your disposal," the Marquess answered, "but you appear to be very busy."

"I am enjoying myself," Harry replied, "and that is definitely what the Doctor advocated after the boredom of life in Cambrai!"

The Marquess knew this was where the Army of Occupation had been billeted. His eyes were twinkling however as he said, "I always understood you spent a great deal of time in Paris."

"As much as I could," Harry admitted.

"With 'the most alluring, the most captivating and the most expensive *Cocottes* in Europe'," the Marquess quoted.

Harry laughed. "They were certainly the most expensive." Then he went upstairs as his Uncle left to drive the short distance to Devonshire House.

Now as the Marquess sat down at the table and waited for what Sir Hubert had to say, he felt somewhat apprehensive. He could not believe that Harry was in debt. He not only paid a great number of his bills, but he had also increased his allowance. He had been able to do this because he had made so much money last year out of the shipping.

Sir Hubert cleared his throat, then he said, "I am afraid, Maurice, this will come as a shock to you, but I have been told on good authority that Harry intends to marry an actress."

The Marquess stiffened.

For a moment it seemed as if he had been turned into stone.

Then he said, "You cannot be serious!"

"I understand that Harry is very serious," Sir Hubert said, "and he intends to break the news to you at any moment."

The Marquess remembered now that Harry had wanted to have a private talk with him, but never in his wildest dreams had he imagined it could be anything like this. "Who is the actress?" he asked.

"Camille Clyde," Sir Hubert replied. "I do not expect you have heard of, or even seen her."

The Marquess had done both. Camille Clyde had made her name as an actress, first in Shakespearean Plays, then she had diverged to Comedy at which she was undoubtedly brilliant.

The Restoration Plays had been revived, and she had played the lead in one after another, and also in some very amusing French plays which, having been a huge success in Paris, had been translated into English.

Camille Clyde had for some time been the talk of the clubs. She was small, not exactly beautiful, but very attractive, with huge sparkling green eyes, and red hair. She had been the talk of the town and was squired by a number of distinguished gentlemen, but it was rumoured that she was very extravagant. Therefore the majority of those on whom she bestowed her favours were older men who were richer. It was not surprising, the Marquess thought, that Harry should want to take her out to dinner, and offer her his "protection" for a short while.

But marriage!

Marriage was an entirely different proposition.

He could hardly believe that Sir Hubert was serious when he said that was Harry's intention.

It seemed a long time before the Marquess asked in a voice that quivered, "How do you know this?"

"Camille Clyde has been boasting at the theatre that she might consider becoming a Countess! One of my friends knows another actress who is in the play in which Camille now stars. He told me what had been said, and I understand the marriage may take place quite soon."

"I cannot believe it!" the Marquess said. It was a blow he had not expected.

Seeing the expression on his face, Sir Hubert put his hand on his arm. "I knew this would upset you," he said.

"Upset me! Do you think I will allow an actress to be the Chatelaine of Stoke Palace? To live in the rooms on which we have expended so much time and money, and to take the place of my mother who was a beautiful and gracious Lady?"

The Marquess's voice quivered with the shock of it. Quite suddenly, he brought his fist down on the table. "I will not allow it! I will prevent it!" he said, "Even if I have to beggar young Harry by taking away all his money!"

"That is something you cannot do," Sir Hubert said quietly. "You remember you made over to him a hundred thousand pounds only last year. It was an irrevocable gift, Maurice."

The Marquess drew in his breath. "Then what can I do? For God's sake, Hubert, what can I do?"

Sir Hubert sat back in his chair.

"I have been asking myself the same question before you arrived," he said. "If I am honest, Maurice, I always imagined that one day Teresa and Harry would meet, and it would be a fitting outcome to our friendship if they fell in love with each other." He paused before he added, "They could live at Stoke Palace, which when the time came would pass on to their children."

"Do you know," the Marquess remarked, "that is something I have also thought about. I saw Teresa last year when she came home for the holidays, and I thought I have never met a girl who was so entrancing, and as you have so often said, she is very much like her mother."

"I do not think Harry has ever seen her," Sir Hubert said.

The Marquess shook his head. "Harry, if you remember, was being entranced with London when he came back from France, and you and Teresa went North almost as soon as he arrived."

"Then what we must do is to get them together," Sir Hubert said. He was speaking in the same voice as when he was planning something new in the shipyard, or when he had a brilliant idea as to where they should invest their money.

"We can do that," the Marquess said, "but how much time have we?"

"That is what worries me," Sir Hubert replied, "but I can find out from my friend what is being planned, and you must insist that Harry comes to Stoke Palace with you."

"I will do anything – anything to prevent this appalling marriage from taking place!" the Marquess said fervently. "How can he contemplate anything that is so likely to be an utter and complete failure?" Sir Hubert did not answer, and the Marquess went on, "Has he no respect for his title, for me, for Stoke, or for his position in society?"

He paused for a moment before he went on more angrily, "Who will receive an actress in their houses, even if she is wearing a coronet on her head?"

As he was speaking, both men were remembering that in the previous century when they were young, the Earl of Derby had married Elizabeth Fallon, who had been the first actress to enter the Peerage. The marriage had caused a tremendous scandal at the time.

"I will not tolerate this! I will not let it occur to *my* name!" the Marquess said as if he had spoken aloud of the Countess of Derby.

"That is exactly how I knew you would feel," Sir Hubert said, "and although Camille Clyde is very pretty, she is undoubtedly what my wife would have called 'common'!"

"I will see her dead first!" the Marquess said furiously, "before she moves into Stoke Palace!"

# CHAPTER TWO

Coming back to London from school, Teresa thought that it was like starting a new chapter in a book.

She had been so busy in her last term because she was determined to please her father by gaining as many prizes as possible. She had in fact been first in English, Foreign Languages and Mathematics, which she knew would delight him.

She had enjoyed her school, outside Bath, where the pupils were from all the most famous families in England.

Teresa had been spoilt because of her father's generosity to the school, and she had been allowed to have her own horse and her own dog with her.

All the girls could ride if they wanted to, but the horses came from a Livery Stable, and as Sir Hubert had said, they were not good enough for Teresa.

She had therefore brought with her a horse which

she adored, and a groom to look after it. She had ridden every morning and, when it was possible, in the afternoon.

None of the girls had been particularly envious. They had realised she was a far better rider than they were. Most of them, when they became débutantes, would either give up riding, or be quite happy to trit-trot in Rotten Row. Few wished to gallop over the countryside.

Teresa had arranged now that *Mercury*, her horse, would go back ahead of her, and she was looking forward to riding him in London.

Her father had told her that she was to make her debut this Season, and he had arranged for the Dowager Countess of Wilton to present her at Court. But Teresa was not greatly excited about it. She thought it would be fun to go to Balls, as the girls at school had talked about them so often.

She, however, was far more interested in being with her father and going with him to Liverpool to see his ships. It was something she had done every holiday, and he had talked to her as if she was a boy, describing the new improvements he had introduced. Also he explained why one ship was faster than another. He talked to her just as he had to her mother: about his business, his plans for the future, and the different companies in which he was interested.

Teresa did not have to pretend. She found everything he told her absorbing, and asked intelligent questions. This was something she had done since she was quite small. "We will go to Liverpool," she told herself as she travelled towards London, "and perhaps Papa will take me on a voyage."

Now that the war was over, the English were pouring into France, and other parts of Europe. Some of the relations of the other girls at school had been to France and Italy, and had come back full of tales, not only of the devastation that had been caused during the fighting, but they described the treasures they had seen in the Museums, Churches and Palaces.

"I must travel, I must!" Teresa told herself. She wondered if her father would be sending his ships into the Mediterranean.

Sitting beside her in the carriage in which she was travelling was *Rufus*, her Spaniel, who went everywhere with her. After some argument with the Headmistress, he was allowed to sit at her feet in the classroom while she did her lessons. He was an intelligent dog and understood that he was not to make a noise, and he never moved until the class was dismissed, but then he jumped about with joy, to the delight of the other pupils.

Now Teresa patted him and smoothed his red-gold coat. She was thinking that what *Rufus* would enjoy more than anything else was being at Globe Hall. She had often teased her father about the name he had given the country house he had bought for her mother in Lancashire which had belonged to a distinguished County family, but it was sold because the heir to the property had been killed early in the war.

The house had carried the owner's name, but Sir

Hubert, with a smile of amusement, had re-christened it Globe Hall.

"Why 'Globe', Papa?" Teresa had asked when she first heard about it.

"Because my ships will eventually encircle the Globe!" Sir Hubert replied. As his ships increased in number it seemed very likely, and the name was therefore appropriate.

Teresa had spent all her holidays at Globe Hall, as Sir Hubert did not think that London was the right place for her until she was grown up. He was well aware that she was very lovely, for every year her beauty increased, and he was made even more worried when he looked at her.

Two words were foremost in his mind – "Fortune-Hunters!" He knew only too well what happened. Heiresses were pursued by irresponsible Bucks and Beau, who had thrown away their fortunes by gambling in the Clubs of St. James's Street. They drank too much and had too little to do. If they came to London with even quite a considerable sum of money, it was soon dissipated on cards and "Cyprians".

The last holiday when Teresa had been at home was Christmas. She had enjoyed every minute she had spent with her father at Globe Hall. They had ridden the excellent horse-flesh that filled his stable, and entertained their friends and relations in the Big House. Teresa had also arranged special treats for the children in the village.

"It has all been such fun, Papa!" she said when she kissed Sir Hubert good-bye. "Thank you, thank you, for the most enjoyable holiday there has ever been."

When she left Sir Hubert was wondering whether, by the end of the year, she would find such simple things amusing. He had already arranged with the Dowager Countess of Wilton that she would give a Ball for Teresa at Stoke Palace. There would also be a Ball in London for which he and the Marquess had made up a long list of distinguished guests.

Sir Hubert was wise enough to realise that because he was so rich, every door in Mayfair would be open to his daughter. What he wanted to avoid were the men who would seek to marry Teresa for her money and not for herself.

She was already very beautiful, and it would be, he thought, impossible for any man not to be moved by her loveliness. She had expressive eyes, a translucent skin and hair which was the pale gold of the dawn. Though she resembled her mother there was something original about her beauty, which Sir Hubert had never seen in any other woman.

The Marquess agreed with him. "Teresa is unique," he said, "and we are going to find it difficult, Hubert, to choose a man who is worthy of her."

"That is what I have been thinking myself," Sir Hubert said, "and whatever happens, we must keep her away from those persistent Fortune-Hunters."

He spoke harshly, for there had just recently been a scandal when a young woman had been married for her money. She had then been cheated out of it by her husband, a dissolute young Peer who had already run through two fortunes.

"Do not worry, Hubert," the Marquess said. "Teresa will have two very fierce watch dogs in you and me!"

Sir Hubert had smiled at the description. At the same time, he was undoubtedly worried.

Teresa, however, was looking forward to her first Season with the excitement of a child who had been told she was to be taken to a pantomime. "It will be thrilling, will it not, *Rufus*?" she said to her Spaniel, "but you will be counting the days when we can go to Globe Hall, and I am almost certain you are right! We shall enjoy that more than dressing up and dancing on a polished floor."

Then she told herself she must appreciate the trouble her father was taking to make certain she was a success. He had asked her to compile a list of the girls with whom she had been at school, and also to add to it any other friends he might have forgotten.

When Teresa looked at her list she was surprised to realise how small it was. When she had been at Globe Hall, she was always with her father, who was so interesting. And she found him so entertaining that she had really paid little attention to any other men she met. She could understand why her mother had adored him. Wherever they went he seemed to stand out so that everyone listened to him.

When Teresa arrived in Berkeley Square, Sir Hubert was waiting for her.

She flung her arms around his neck saying, "I am

home, Papa! I am home! Now I never have to leave you again!"

"It is wonderful to see you, my dearest," her father said.

"I have such a lot to tell you," Teresa smiled, "and three prizes to show you."

She thought her father was impressed, and she was still talking about her achievements as they went into the Drawing Room. "You have two new pictures!" Teresa exclaimed. "I love the one over the mantelpiece."

"I thought you would appreciate it," her father said, "and there is a Stubbs in my Study which I am sure will also please you."

"I want to see everything, hear exactly why you bought them, and what they cost," Teresa said. She stretched out her arms and exclaimed, "Oh, Papa, it is so wonderful to be home! To know I do not have to go back to school and can be with you."

She paused a moment before she added, "If I was your son, you would now be taking me into the business, showing me how you run it, and letting me help you. But whether I am a boy or a girl, that is what I want to do!"

Sir Hubert laughed. "My dearest," he said, "you are going to be the Belle of the Season."

Teresa made a little murmur of protest. "That means that a lot of people will look at me, and girls of my own age will dislike me! I would be much happier, Papa, working with you."

"I have worked hard for years," Sir Hubert

answered, "so that your mother should have anything and everything she desired, then, when I lost her, I worked for you."

His voice had deepened when he spoke of his wife. Teresa was aware of the pain it cause him. Then he went on quickly, "I want you to have the most beautiful gowns, the finest horses, in fact anything your heart desires."

"Darling Papa, you would say something like that!" Teresa replied, "but you have forgotten something."

"What is that?" Sir Hubert asked.

"When you and Mama made me, she gave me her looks and you gave me your brain!"

Sir Hubert stared at his daughter in surprise. "My brain?" he said slowly.

"Of course that is what you have done," Teresa said. "They said at school, first behind my back, then to my face, that I had a man's brain, which was a mistake in a woman. And of course, that is your fault."

Sir Hubert laughed. "I have been accused of many things in my life," he exclaimed, "but this is the first time I have been accused of producing a too-clever child!"

"The trouble is, you see," Teresa said, "I get bored when things are too easy. I need to struggle to get things right. I want to fight, as you fought, to possess what is worth having."

"You astound me!" Sir Hubert answered, "and it is something, my dearest daughter, I have never thought about before."

"Well, just think," Teresa said, "what fun it would

be if I could help you to control your ships, make plans for new contracts, visit new countries, and invent new improvements. I promise you, I shall be just as good as any young man you might wish to have as your assistant!"

Because it was something he had never anticipated and seemed almost revolutionary, Sir Hubert did not reply.

The next day, Teresa went shopping with the Dowager Countess.

When they were alone Sir Hubert told the Marquess what she had said to him.

"That is certainly unusual!" the Marquess observed when he had listened. "But I suppose, Hubert, it is something you might have expected. If you had had a son, he would obviously have been brilliant, like you, and it would be impossible for any daughter of yours to have a beautiful face and nothing behind it."

"That is all very well," Sir Hubert complained, "but she is bound to be critical of the men who wish to marry her."

"And a good thing too!" the Marquess said. "Some of these young hobbledehoys have no more brains than an earthworm and I certainly would not trust them with my money!"

Even as he spoke he knew he had made a mistake. There was a frown on his friend's forehead as once again he was thinking of the Fortune-Hunters. It was then as they looked at each other, that the same thought struck both men.

"Wellington was very pleased with Harry," the Marquess said after a pregnant silence. "He told me that if he had remained in the Army he would eventually make an exceptionally fine General."

"But you told me he insisted upon resigning," Sir Hubert replied.

"That was the Army of Occupation," the Marquess explained. "It might have been necessary. But it was bad for all those young men to have little or nothing to do, and even the allurements of Paris grew stale after a while."

Sir Hubert did not reply. He was thinking that Harry had merely exchanged the allurements of one capital for another.

Nonetheless, he was now twenty-seven and certainly would not be a Fortune-Hunter. As his Guardian, the Marquess had invested Harry's money as well as his own on the advice of Sir Hubert.

The Marquess was now an exceedingly rich man. When his fortune was added to his Nephew's, there would be no reason for Harry to marry for money. But what he must not do was marry an actress.

To do so would not only break his Uncle's heart, but also be an insult to his place in the Peerage and the family of which he was now the head.

Aloud Sir Hubert spoke the words which were already in the Marquess's mind. "We will go to Stoke Palace on Friday," he said.

"I will make Harry come with us," the Marquess answered.

* * *

When she was told they were going to Stoke Palace, Teresa was delighted. "Do you realise, Papa," she said, "because we always went home for the holidays, I have never seen Stoke. In my mind it has always been a Fairytale Palace, and it kept recurring in my dreams."

"Now you will see it," her father said, "and I am sure it will delight you! You have no idea how hard the Marquess and I have worked to make it as perfect as it was when it was first built."

He knew that Teresa was listening, and he went on, "We scoured England to find the furniture that had belonged there over the ages. I think you will also appreciate the Picture Gallery, which is the Marquess's most precious hobby and which I am actually convinced is better than any gallery in London!"

"I can hardly wait until Friday, so as to see it all, and by that time I shall have some of the beautiful gowns which the Countess has chosen for me."

She laughed before she said, "She is so sweet to me, Papa, and says that buying my clothes is as exciting as if she was buying them for herself. Because her family was poor when she was young, they had to skimp and save for her to have just two pretty gowns in which to make her début."

"But she married a rich man," Sir Hubert said.

"They fell in love with each other the very night they met," Teresa said, "and the Countess told me how happy she was until he died last year." Her voice dropped as she added, "I think, Papa, one of the reasons why the Marquess has asked her to chaperon me is because it has given her something else to think about besides the loss of her husband."

The compassion in Teresa's voice was very moving, and her father said, "Do what you can, my dearest, to cheer her up and of course we are very grateful to her for saying she will present you."

"I only hope I do not disappoint you, Papa!" Teresa said, "I know you have told me that I shall be a great success. It will be too humiliating if, when I do appear, nobody takes any notice of me!"

"You need not worry about that," Sir Hubert said.

Some cynical part of his brain was provoking him. Even if the social world were not bowled over by Teresa's beauty they would be thinking, as his only child, how exceedingly rich she was!

The Marquess was busy making arrangements for their visit to Stoke Palace. Teresa was shopping in the country and Sir Hubert went to Tattersall's Salesrooms, where he had heard there were some very fine horses coming up for sale and when he saw them he was not disappointed.

He bought six without even noticing that they were extremely expensive, and arranged for them to be taken to Stoke Palace immediately. He thought that this would certainly be an inducement for Harry to come down for the weekend. Even if he had been thinking of doing something quite different, the horses would be an indubitable attraction.

He was just leaving Tattersall's when he saw a

friend, Lord Charles Graham who had told him of Harry's intention to marry Camille Clyde.

He was inspecting one of the horses that had not been in the Sale, and Sir Hubert walked across the yard and put his hand on Lord Charles's shoulder.

"I expected to see you here, Charles," he said.

"Hello, Hubert," his friend replied. "I suppose, as I am late, you have picked all the best cherries off the tree!"

"I shall be extremely annoyed if I have missed any!" Sir Hubert replied. His friend laughed. "I am wanting a new mount for the winter. And of course, I have arrived too late for this Sale, at any rate."

"I wanted to see you," Sir Hubert said.

"About what?" Lord Charles enquired.

They walked a little to one side of the other people in the yard. "You know what you told me about Harry Lanbourne?" Sir Hubert asked. "Is it still true that he intends to marry that woman?"

"It is funny you should say that," his friend replied. "I was with Rosie last night. She has a small part in the play in which Camille Clyde is appearing."

Sir Hubert nodded. He knew this was where Lord Charles had originally obtained the information about Harry. "Did she tell you anything new?" he asked.

"She said that Camille had made up her mind to accept Harry."

Sir Hubert drew in his breath. "You are sure of that?"

"My girl-friend is her confidante, and is also very

envious of her. I suppose after this it will be the ambition of every pretty creature who walks the boards to shine in the Peerage."

Sir Hubert was frowning and moved a little closer to his friend. "Now listen, Charles," he said, "I must know if you have any idea of when this marriage might take place."

Charles shrugged his shoulders. "If my girl-friend had been aware of it she would have told me," he said, "but she is absolutely certain that Camille is now determined to marry young Lanbourne. If you ask my opinion, I think he is a fool!"

"So do I," Sir Hubert said.

He did not waste any more time, but hurried away from Tattersall's. He could only hope, as he went to find the Marquess, that the marriage would not take place before the weekend.

Harry had promised his Uncle that he would come to Stoke Palace, and he hoped the young man would keep his word. He then remembered that he had an appointment with a sea-captain who had just arrived in England from a long voyage to China and the East.

Sir Hubert had actually forgotten about it in his anxiety to buy some horses for the Marquess. Now he recalled that he had told his Secretary to get in touch with the captain whose name was Chang-Mai.

Sir Hubert promised to call on him some time during the day, but he could not say the exact hour. As he stepped into his carriage he drew from his waist-coat pocket the address that his Secretary had given him. When he read it he raised his eyebrows and smiled. Knowing the Chinaman was an old rascal in many ways, he was not surprised that his address was in Chinatown. He was thinking he would be very surprised if this particular ship had not carried a number of illegal goods.

There was always a good market in Chinatown for them. Things such as jewellery, Oriental treasures, precious stones and talismans. Not to mention, Sir Hubert told himself, drugs.

There was always an abundance of eager purchasers of opium and cocaine for which Chinatown was famous. "I wonder what he has brought me this time," Sir Hubert thought.

He had asked the captain when he set out a year ago to bring him back anything he thought he would appreciate.

"What Your Excellency ask for," the Chinaman had replied, "making hole in pocket!"

"I do not mind several holes, if you bring me what I want," Sir Hubert replied.

He had a strong suspicion that many of the things Chang-Mai had brought back to England in the past had been stolen.

Isolated Temples were invariably fair game. Monasteries whose treasures had been guarded ferociously over the centuries sometimes grew lax.

Sir Hubert was wise enough not to ask too many questions. He was content to add to his collections some exquisite statues of the Buddha, one of which was carved out of a whole emerald.

There were also pearls which had come to Bombay from the Gulf, and when his wife wore them, she was the envy of every other woman in the room.

He was sure now that what the Chinaman had waiting for him in Chinatown would be well worth having.

The Marquess, standing at the window of his house, saw a phaeton drive up to the front door. He knew it contained Harry, but he had not expected him back this afternoon, although he had hoped to see him later in the evening.

It suddenly occurred to him that it would be a great mistake if Harry told him now what was in his mind before, as they had planned, he came to Stoke Palace and met Teresa. The Marquess therefore walked across the room, and stood in front of the fireplace, holding some papers in his hands.

A few minutes later the door opened and Harry came in. The Marquess thought he was looking extremely handsome, and rather pleased with himself. Because he was afraid of what he might say, the Marquess said quickly, "Oh, there you are, Harry. I am glad you have come as I am just going out. But I wanted to tell you it is important that you should come to Stoke tomorrow."

He thought there was a look of consternation in Harry's face, or it might have been a trick of the light. With a slightly questioning note in his voice he asked, "Why is it important, Uncle Maurice?"

"Sir Hubert has given you and me a very generous present," the Marquess replied. "He heard that Feversham's horses were for sale, and has gone to Tattersall's this afternoon to buy them for us."

"Feversham's horses?" Harry exclaimed. "I had heard they were being sold, but understood that the prices they expected was outrageous, and therefore did not trouble to go."

"Well, Sir Hubert said that he would give them to us. It would appear very ungrateful if we were not waiting at Stoke when they arrive."

"But of course," Harry agreed. "I shall certainly look forward to riding them." He gave a sigh. "If you ask me, Uncle Maurice, only Sir Hubert could afford them."

"I agree with you there," the Marquess said. "And Feversham would not sell them if he had not made a mess of his affairs which, if you ask me, was sheer stupidity."

"Well, it has certainly turned out to our advantage," Harry said. "I am extremely grateful to Sir Hubert for adding to your stable, which is already a very fine one, as I do not have to tell you."

"That is the sort of compliment I like!" the Marquess said.

There was a little pause and he had the feeling that Harry was about to confide in him. Quickly, he glanced down at the papers in his hand and said, "I am late! I am sorry I cannot stay and talk to you now about the latest addition to our possessions at Stoke, but I promised to be with the Duke half-an-hour ago."

He walked towards the door and as he reached it Harry asked, "Will you be in for dinner, Uncle Maurice?"

"Not tonight," the Marquess replied.

As he reached the hall he saw to his relief that his carriage was waiting outside. When he stepped into it he was determined to go to White's Club, where he hoped there would be some of his friends who would be able to tell him a little more about Harry and his appalling intention to marry an actress.

The Marquess's carriage went up Berkeley Street and into Piccadilly. He found himself unexpectedly praying that by some miracle he would be able to prevent Harry from ruining his life.

# CHAPTER THREE

Sir Hubert arrived back at his house in Berkeley Square at nearly seven o'clock. When he walked into the hall the Butler said, "His Lordship's in the Study, Sir."

Thinking that there must be something wrong, as the Marquess had called unexpectedly at such a late hour, Sir Hubert hurried to his Study. The Marquess was there reading a newspaper, which he put down as Sir Hubert appeared.

"You are very late coming home! I was wondering what had happened to you."

"I have been to Chinatown," Sir Hubert replied, "and I have brought back some exciting purchases to show you."

He put the parcel he was carrying down on a table and said, "I presume you have something to tell me."

"I have," the Marquess answered in a heavy voice, "but I want to see your treasures first."

"I think it is more important that we should have a drink," Sir Hubert said.

He walked across to the grog-table and poured out two glasses of the Marquess's favourite champagne which was in an ice-cooler.

"I thought somehow," he said as he did so, "that you would need this tonight, and so I told the servants to put it on ice."

"You are very kind," the Marquess said, still in a heavy tone.

Sir Hubert poured himself out a glass. Then he went to the table on which he had put down his parcel. It was roughly packed, but he undid it carefully, and lifted from it an exquisite effigy of Krishna, the Hindu God of Love, which had been sculpted in gold and set with a variety of different precious stones.

"I like that!" the Marquess said as Sir Hubert stood it up on the table.

It suddenly struck Sir Hubert that it was not very tactful at this particular moment to be showing the Marquess the God of Love. He therefore hurriedly brought something else from his package.

This was an elephant in pink quartz, holding his trunk above his head, in which was set a large and perfect pearl.

The Marquess looked at it with delight. "I cannot think," he said, "how your Chinese sea-captain whom you have often described to me, has such amazing good taste."

"I suspect he has been educated by centuries of ancestors," Sir Hubert answered. "I think you will enjoy the third thing he has brought me, which is another treasure to add to my collection."

He produced a Bodhisattva, carved and painted in wood, and told the Marquess it was from the Sung Dynasty in about AD 960. The wood was not cracked and the colours were unfaded.

Sir Hubert was looking at it with delight when the Marquess asked, "Is that all?"

"I think it is quite enough for the moment," Sir Hubert replied. "There is one thing more, but I will tell you about that later."

He produced from the bottom of the package a small bottle. He set it down beside the three beautiful objects on the table. The Marquess looked at it curiously, but before he could speak Sir Hubert said, "Now, Maurice, it is your turn. What has happened?"

"I went to White's Club," the Marquess replied, "to avoid Harry who I felt was going to tell me about his intended marriage. When I got to the Club, I found there was every reason for him to do so."

"Why?" Sir Hubert asked.

"I saw your friend Lord Charles Graham there, and he told me what he had said to you at Tattersall's."

"I was going to tell you myself," Sir Hubert remarked.

"To make quite sure I was not mistaken," the Marquess went on, "I promised Graham to call on his actress friend Rosie to find out if she had any further information."

Seeing the expression on his friend's face, Sir Hubert knew that Rosie obviously had. "What did she say?" he asked when the Marquess was silent.

"I waited outside in the carriage while Graham went into her flat," the Marquess replied, "and when he did so, he told me there had been a rehearsal at the theatre this morning, and when it was over, Camille Clyde had boasted that she intended to be married on either Sunday night, or Monday morning."

"Did she ask anyone to her wedding?" Sir Hubert asked after a pause.

The Marquess shook his head. "No, she told Graham that it was a secret. She would give a party after the wedding had taken place to which they would all be present to drink her health."

The Marquess's voice seemed to crack on the last words. Then he asked, "For God's sake, Hubert, tell me what I should do!"

"I have the answer ready," Sir Hubert said quietly, "and now you must listen very carefully to what I have planned."

"I am very excited!" Teresa said to her father.

They had set off after luncheon on Friday to drive to Stoke Palace. They were alone in Sir Hubert's new and very smart phaeton, of which he was exceedingly proud. The Marquess and Harry were travelling in another phaeton that had left before luncheon.

"The sooner I get the boy away from London the

better!" the Marquess said. "I have asked him to drive my carriage which, as it is drawn by three horses, will prevent him from thinking of anything else on the way down."

Sir Hubert thought this was a good idea, and he was also delighted to be alone with his daughter. He told her in detail about how much he had contributed to the design of the new phaeton. This included the size of the wheels and the lightness of the body.

"When it is drawn by the right horses," he said, "I would defy anyone I race in this vehicle to beat me!"

Teresa laughed.

"You always win, Papa."

"That is what I hope I shall do this weekend," Sir Hubert said.

"Doing what?" Teresa enquired.

"That is what I am going to tell you, my dearest," Sir Hubert answered, "and I need your help."

"You have obviously got something up your sleeve," Teresa said, "and I am sure, Papa, it is something thrilling."

"I hope you will think so," Sir Hubert replied in a somewhat mysterious tone.

She glanced at him from under her eye lashes, wondering what he was planning. She always knew when her father was concentrating on something very special. He had a different look about him from that which he had at other times.

She thought, as she had often thought before, how handsome he was. Even the few grey hairs he now had at the sides of his temples added to his looks.

"Well, first of all," she said lightly, "let me congratulate you on the phaeton! You must certainly find someone to race us, just so that you can show them that once again you are a winner."

Sir Hubert laughed. "You will see one more innovation I have not yet shown you," he said. "There is a special place on each side of the phaeton for pistols."

"I suppose," Teresa said, "you are thinking of Highwaymen, but I cannot believe that any 'Gentlemen of the Road' would attempt to hold up this smart vehicle."

"One never knows," Sir Hubert replied, "and since the end of the war there have been a lot more Highwaymen than ever before."

"I suppose they are men who have come back to England to find there is no employment for them," Teresa said in a quiet voice, "and nobody is in the least grateful for the years they spent fighting for England."

"I am afraid that is true," Sir Hubert agreed. "It is an absolute disgrace that the men leaving the Army are dismissed without a pension. Even those who are injured are left to beg from passers-by, or starve."

"Has nobody made a fuss about this in the Houses of Parliament?" Teresa enquired.

"A few speeches have been made," Sir Hubert replied scornfully, "but nobody has paid any attention to them."

"I quite see, Papa," Teresa said, "that you will have

to go into Parliament. If you were there, they would be forced to listen to you."

Sir Hubert smiled. "I think, on the whole, I prefer my ships."

"And so do I," Teresa said. "That brings us back to the question of whether you will allow me to help you in the same way I would be able to do if I had been a boy?"

"You can help me in a very different way at the moment," Sir Hubert answered. "It will be interesting to see if you are clever enough to do exactly as I want you to do."

"That is a challenge which I accept with both hands," Teresa said. "What is it you want?"

Sir Hubert was driving without a groom on the seat behind. There was therefore no need for him to lower his voice. Instead, in a very firm tone, he said, "I want you to save young Harry Lanbourne from making an absolute fool of himself, and from making his Uncle the most miserable man on earth."

"What has the Earl done?" Teresa asked. "I have never met him, strange though it may seem, but he was always held up to me as being an example of everything that was perfect."

Her father did not speak, and she went on, "When Harry was commended by the Duke of Wellington, you were as excited about it as the Marquess! I remember feeling very envious that being a woman I could not go to war and gain a medal for gallantry."

"I never thought of you being jealous of anyone," Sir Hubert said, "but now that you put it like that, I see it must have been annoying to have Harry described to you as the acme of everything that was perfect!"

"I suppose," Teresa answered, "it made me more determined than ever to be a success at school, so that you would be proud of *me*."

"Which I have always been, my dearest," Sir Hubert said quickly.

They drove on for a little while before Teresa said, "So tell me – what has Harry done?"

"The Marquess is distraught," Sir Hubert said, "because I learned from one of my friends that Harry intends to marry an actress called Camille Clyde."

"I have heard of her!" Teresa exclaimed. "She came to Bath soon after I went to school there. She was playing in *Romeo and Juliet*. Some of the older girls were taken to see her and they said she was wonderful!"

"I believe she is a good actress," Sir Hubert admitted. "At the same time, as you will understand, it would kill the Marquess if his Nephew and Heir puts a woman from the stage in place of his mother."

"I suppose a lot of people would be shocked," Teresa agreed, "but if he loves her, it must be very difficult not to ask her to be his wife."

Sir Hubert could not at first find the words to answer this. Then he said, "What a young Gentleman like Harry feels for an actress is not the same as what he feels for the woman he wishes to marry."

Teresa thought about this for a moment. Then she said, "Are you suggesting, Papa, that Camille Clyde is like Nell Gwyn who was on the stage, and of whom

King Charles II was very fond, but of course he could not marry her."

"Yes, that is exactly what I am trying to say," Sir Hubert said in a tone of relief.

"But King Charles already had a wife," Teresa answered, "so that it was impossible for him to marry Nell Gwyn, although he loved her very much."

"Even if Charles II had not been married," Sir Hubert said, "he would not have married Nell Gwyn, and it is something Harry cannot do either."

"Even though he . . loves Camille Clyde?"

"Not in any circumstances!" Sir Hubert said firmly.

"But, perhaps . . if she loves him he . . does not want to . . make her . . very unhappy," Teresa argued.

"There are plenty of other men to console her, just as there have been in the past," Sir Hubert said sharply.

"Are you saying, Papa, that she has been in love before?" Teresa asked.

"Quite a number of times," Sir Hubert replied.

Teresa thought this over, then she said, "In that case, Harry must not marry her, because if she became bored at being a Countess which at first would be very exciting for her, she might also become bored with Harry and find somebody else to love."

Sir Hubert breathed an inward sigh of relief. His daughter, in an ingenious way, had worked the situation out for herself. He was well aware how innocent Teresa was, but even so she was an avid reader and had won a prize for History. He thought she must have some idea of what a mistress meant.

She would also realise there was the difference between a woman of no importance and a man's wife, who bore his name. Quickly, because he thought it was a mistake to talk too much about this part of Harry's problem, he said, "What I want you to do, my dearest, is to save Harry from marrying Camille Clyde, which the Marquess has been told on excellent authority may happen either on Sunday night, or Monday morning."

"A secret marriage?" Teresa exclaimed. "I am sure that would be very exciting."

"It is something which must not take place!" Sir Hubert thundered. "You know how much Stoke Palace means to the Marquess and how proud he is of his family tree."

Teresa nodded and her father went on, "Harry is his Heir and for him to make a *mésalliance* would destroy everything the Marquess has worked for and cared about, ever since I have known him."

Teresa laid her hand on her father's knee.

"I know, Papa, it was entirely due to you that the Marquess was able to make enough money to restore the Palace, and also to buy back his house in Berkeley Square."

"He is my best friend," Sir Hubert said, "and you know I am very fond of him. That is why, my Dearest, we have to help him."

"Of course we must," Teresa agreed, "so tell me what I have to do."

"It is quite simple." Sir Hubert said. "You have to marry Harry!"

Teresa turned to stare at him and he said quickly, "It will only be a sham wedding, but Harry has to believe it is real."

"I do not understand what you are .. saying," Teresa complained. "How will he want to .. marry me if he is .. in love with .. Camille Clyde?"

"Now, listen very carefully to what I have to tell you," her father answered, "for if anything goes wrong with the plan, it could be disastrous for the Marquess and we will never be able to forgive ourselves."

"I understand that .. of course I understand," Teresa said. "What I cannot see is how what .. you suggest is .. possible."

"I have trusted you," Sir Hubert said, "with my plans for my business, some of which are very secret until they are successful, and some of which are extremely difficult to achieve."

"I realise that, Papa," Teresa agreed.

"The first thing," her father began as he drove on, "is for you and Harry to try out the horses I have just bought at Tattersall's, and which I understand are the best in the whole country."

"I shall certainly enjoy every minute of that!" Teresa smiled.

"You must realise," Sir Hubert went on, "that a young man of Harry's age – he is twenty-seven – is not particularly interested in very young girls. I have heard his Uncle say that he is bored still by débutantes and never speaks to them if he can avoid it."

"But .. you think .. I can .. interest him?" Teresa asked bluntly.

"That is entirely up to you," her father answered. "I have always found you extremely intelligent and the best companion in the world, with the exception of your mother. I want you to try and make Harry notice you, enjoy being with you and of course, if it is possible, fall in love with you."

To his surprise, Teresa threw back her head and laughed. "Oh, really Papa!" she said. "I think you are asking too much! If Harry intends to be married on Sunday how could all this happen in two days and two nights?"

"Stranger things have happened," Sir Hubert remarked. "All I am asking you to do is to try."

"And if, which is extremely unlikely, he finds me – who has only just stopped being a schoolgirl – more attractive than Camille Clyde," Teresa said, "are you expecting him to go down on one knee and beg me to be his wife?"

"That is too much to expect," Sir Hubert conceded, "and so I have arranged with the Marquess that you and Harry will be 'married', although of course it will be only a pretence."

"I do not .. understand," Teresa pleaded.

"I have just received, as you know, some new treasures from the East," Sir Hubert began.

"I know, and I think they are absolutely wonderful!" Teresa interrupted. "Especially the elephant.

And you did say, Papa, that I could have it in my Sitting-Room."

"You can have it and everything else I have bought," her father replied, "if you can pull off this coup, which I know will be very difficult, but one of the most rewarding plans I have ever attempted."

"Tell me how it is . . possible," Teresa begged.

"I received the three treasures which you have admired, from my Chinese captain," Sir Hubert said, "and then I asked him half-jokingly, what drugs he had brought back with him."

"'Dangerous question, Excellency, no wish answer,' he said.

"'I am just interested,' I replied.

"'Chang-Mai show something never seen afore,' he whispered."

"What was it?" Teresa asked.

"He produced a small bottle," Her father replied, "and told me it was something they had just perfected in Peking after a great deal of research."

"A drug?" Teresa asked.

"A very strange one. Apparently when a man takes it, it immediately numbs his brain. He can walk, talk and obey everything that is said to him, but he is not actually thinking because, to put it simply, his brain has been anaesthetised."

"I think that sounds extraordinary, but clever!" Teresa said.

"That is what I thought," Sir Hubert agreed, "Chang-Mai called in a boy, gave him a glass of wine to drink into which he put two drops of the special drug."

"What happened?" Teresa asked breathlessly.

"The boy appeared quite normal, but he did not speak unless he was told what to say. Chang-Mai made him say: 'Good-morning, Sir, very nice day,' and 'Good-night, Sir, I now go bed.' He repeated the words in a normal voice, completely unaware of what he was doing."

"How extraordinary," Teresa exclaimed.

Sir Hubert went on:

"He then told the boy to sit down in a chair, which he did – to shut his eyes and go to sleep."

"And he did that?" Teresa asked.

"When I left he was asleep, and Chang-Mai assured me that in an hour's time he would wake up with no idea what had happened."

"I can hardly believe it!" Teresa said. "It is certainly extraordinary, Papa! And of course, I realise that is what you intend to give to Harry."

"It is the only way we can save him," Sir Hubert replied, "but you must forgive me, my lovely daughter, for involving you in this."

"But . . what happens . . after he . . wakes?" Teresa asked slowly.

"That of course is the difficult part," Sir Hubert admitted. "We have to tell him that he is married, and to you."

"But . . suppose he . . is furious . . and very . . angry with me?"

"He may be that," Sir Hubert said, "but knowing

Harry, I think he will control his feelings, and not be too unpleasant about it."

Teresa gave a little shiver. "I do . . not like . . it, Papa," she said.

"But you realise," her father assured her, "that it is only a question of time before we tell him it was all a hoax. And the wedding, which must take place to make it credible will be performed by an actor playing the part of the Parson."

"Oh, I thought you intended to tell Harry at once that he had been . . deceived," Teresa remarked.

"Now work that out for yourself," her father replied. "If, on Sunday night, we tell him it was a hoax, there is nothing to stop him from marrying Camille Clyde on Monday morning, which is what she wants. Or for that matter any other day of the week."

Teresa looked at her father in astonishment.

"Are you really suggesting, Papa, that we keep up this pretence for a long time?"

"I see no other way that we can prevent Harry from marrying this woman," Sir Hubert said, "and with any luck, she will be so annoyed at him throwing her over at the last moment, that she will merely transfer her attentions to some other poor fool who is enamoured of her because she is behind the footlights."

There was silence until they had gone some way before Sir Hubert said, "I am sorry if I have upset you. Perhaps it would be better to try and get somebody else to play the part." Sir Hubert paused and then continued, "But trusting a stranger in what is a very personal family secret is always risky and also it would be impossible for a stranger not to talk of what happened."

There was no need for Sir Hubert to stress this point. Teresa knew only too well how, because her father was so rich and so successful, the Press were always following him about. They wrote in the newspapers about everything he was doing. They reiterated over and over again how much money he had and how much more he had since the last time they wrote about him.

Very much the same thing happened to the Marquess. His name was mentioned almost daily in the Court Circular of every newspaper. He also continued to be the joy and delight of the gossip-mongers.

They drove a little further in silence.

Then at last Teresa said:

"I will do it, Papa . . but you will have to help me . . I could not . . bear to let you or the . . Marquess down."

"Thank you, my dearest," Sir Hubert answered.

They drove on in silence.

# CHAPTER FOUR

When Teresa first saw Stoke Palace she was speechless. She had learned that it was magnificent and impressive because she had heard about it so often. But she had no idea it would be quite so large, or appear to have stepped straight out of a Fairytale.

It shimmered in the sunshine, and the Marquess's standard was flying from the tallest tower. She could hardly believe that it was real. She knew of course that it had been built by Vanbrugh, who had been the architect both for Blenheim Palace and Castle Howard.

The Marquess of the day – in 1726 – was determined to be more important than the Duke of Marlborough, who had been given Blenheim Palace by a grateful Nation. The Marquess therefore gave Vanbrugh carte blanche to do what he considered was really outstanding.

Vanbrugh was delighted. He had experienced some very difficult and unpleasant years with Sarah, the Duchess of Marlborough. She had disliked him and fought him over every plan and, as he said himself, over practically every brick that was laid at Blenheim.

He was therefore pleased to be given a free hand. His imagination had conjured up the most fantastic building it was possible to create, and the Marquess was delighted when people were so impressed by it.

Sir Hubert talked about the Palace to Teresa until they arrived at the front door.

The Marquess and Harry greeted them from the top of the steps. It seemed extraordinary that this was the first time that Teresa had ever met Harry, especially as Sir Hubert was so involved with Stoke Palace. In fact seldom a day passed that he and the Marquess were not in communication with each other.

Teresa appreciated the warmth in the Marquess's voice when he greeted his friend saying, "Hubert! I am delighted to see you!"

"And I am delighted to be here!" Sir Hubert replied. "How are you Harry? I hear you have been enjoying yourself in London after being so bored towards the end of your time in France."

Teresa was looking at Harry as her father spoke. She thought that he was even more good-looking than she had expected after all she had been told about him. She had been sure he would be unusual, but not as handsome in a particularly masculine way. He was broad-shouldered and had the narrow hips of an athlete, and she knew without being told that he was as good a horseman as his Uncle boasted him to be.

"Come in! Come in!" the Marquess invited. "As this is Teresa's first visit, we have a great deal to show her."

"I trust the horses have arrived safely?" Sir Hubert asked Harry.

"Yes, Sir Hubert, and I am extremely grateful to you," Harry replied. "They are appreciating their very comfortable stable which my Uncle tells me were built from your plans."

"I left the Palace to him, but I do know more about stables than he does!"

"I am not certain which is the more luxurious!" Harry laughed.

They went into the Palace and Teresa was immediately impressed by the Great Hall, which had two tiers of diamond-paned windows rising to a magnificently painted ceiling, where a profusion of cupids flitted around Venus. Teresa thought without seeing more that this made it the most unusual building she had ever imagined.

Later she was to be thrilled by the State Dining-Room and the Library, where the Marquess had already collected nearly a thousand books.

At the moment, as they were walking into the Drawing Room, Harry said, "I have heard a great deal about you, Teresa."

"Not half as much as I have heard about you," Teresa replied, "and I made up my mind long ago that if everything that was said was true, you could not be real, but merely the hero out of an adventure story."

Harry laughed. "I assure you, I am very real, especially when I have a chance of riding the marvellous horses that your father has sent us."

"I am looking forward to riding them too," Teresa said.

She saw Harry look at her and knew he was thinking they would be too much for her to handle. She therefore said quickly, "It is what I have every intention of doing, if you are thinking of opposing me."

"I would not dare to do such a thing," Harry retorted. "But they are still young, and they undoubtedly need a firm hand."

Teresa smiled. Because she was small, a number of people had thought that she should have something quiet and docile to ride. But what she really enjoyed was a horse that was difficult, and those which her father had just purchased, being very highly-bred, were certain to be.

She did not wish to argue with Harry, but somehow, as her father had suggested, to make him aware of her. "I will tell you what I would like to do," she said. "After we have had luncheon, perhaps we could ride the horses, providing they are not too tired."

"They arrived yesterday," Harry said, "and although it was a long journey, they have had a good rest with a lot of people tending them."

"Then please let us ride them," Teresa pleaded.

She knew he was doubtful that she could manage, and he replied, "Perhaps you would like to have a look at what else my Uncle has in the stable?"

"Are you refusing the challenge I have offered you?" Teresa asked. "I was going to suggest to Papa, because he would enjoy it so much, that tomorrow we have a competition, over the jumps which I hear he has erected on the new Racecourse he is building for your Uncle."

"You seem to know more about it than I do!" Harry complained. "I had no idea he was going to have a Racecourse."

"Of course he is," Teresa said. "You must exercise yourself properly when you are in the country."

Harry's eyes twinkled. "Now you are rebuking me as my Uncle has done for staying so long in London!" he said. "But I find it very amusing after being abroad for so long."

He paused then added, "And Englishwomen are undoubtedly very pretty!"

He was looking at her in a complimentary manner. She was sure, however, that he was thinking of the beautiful red-headed Camille Clyde.

"That is true," she agreed. "But I have always been told we are not so witty or so clever as our French counterparts."

Harry had obviously not thought of this before. She noticed he thought it over before he replied, "Perhaps it is a mistake for a beautiful woman to be clever. She would be continually contradicting anything one said."

"She might also be stimulating a man to do more,"

Teresa said, "and inspiring him to get to the top of his particular profession."

She hesitated for a moment. Then, lowering her voice so that her father would not hear her, she said, "That is what my mother did, and my father's huge success was, I assure you, in many ways due to her."

She thought Harry looked surprised. Then, in case he should think she was preaching to him, she looked around the room they had just entered. Before he could say anything she exclaimed with delight at the pictures, which were certainly impressive.

Teresa had learnt so much about Art, both from her mother and at school. She was therefore able to repeat little anecdotes about the Artists. She also commented on each one's particular style of painting, and was aware that what she said surprised Harry.

When they went into luncheon, Teresa was thrilled as she examined the tapestries hanging on two of the walls. She congratulated the Marquess on the beautiful chairs. She remembered her father had bought them back from someone who had purchased them over twenty years ago.

The Marquess took her appreciation as a compliment. "You have been very clever, My Lord," she said, "in making it look exactly as Vanbrugh intended."

"I like to think that is so," the Marquess replied, "but, why have you suddenly become so formal? I have always been 'Uncle Maurice' to you until now."

"I know that," Teresa smiled, "but as I have only

just met your Nephew, I thought he might think I was trepassing on his preserves."

They laughed at this and Harry said, "I am delighted to share Uncle Maurice with you, as long as you do not take Stoke Palace away from me."

"I will try not to do that," Teresa answered. "And I would like to show you my home, or perhaps what you would fancy more, Papa's ships."

"Now that is something I really would enjoy!" Harry answered.

"Then you must come with us to Liverpool," Sir Hubert said, "and I will take you on a grand tour of my fleet."

"I shall keep you to your promise," Harry replied.

Luncheon was delicious. When it was finished Teresa ran upstairs to change into her riding-habit. She realised everything had gone well so far, and her father and the Marquess were pleased with her.

When she came downstairs she found the three Gentlemen in the Library. The Marquess was showing them a new picture he had hung over the mantelpiece. This had come up for sale at Christies, and he had thought it would be eminently suitable to add to his collection.

Teresa admired the picture, then she looked at Harry. "I want to be out in the sunshine," she said, "and to see the horses about which Papa is so enthusiastic."

"I will come with you tomorrow," Sir Hubert said, "because now the Marquess and I have some further plans to discuss, so you two young people go ahead."

"The horses are at the front door," Harry said, "but in case, Teresa, you have changed your mind, I have ordered them also to bring one of the other horses on which you can have a very good ride."

"I know exactly what you are saying, in a somewhat under-handed way!" Teresa replied, "but I insist that being a woman I have first choice of the horse I wish to ride."

Harry made a hopeless gesture with his hand. It told her he thought she was merely being obstinate.

The horses that had come from Tattersall's were certainly outstanding. At a quick glance Teresa appreciated that the horse Harry had chosen for her was exceedingly well-bred. But it was quiet and not at all obstreperous like the other two. The grooms in fact had difficulty in holding those.

Teresa chose the one that was bucking furiously. Despite a murmur of protest from Harry, she managed to be lifted into the saddle. She picked up the reins and settled down. She knew she would enjoy what would be a tussle between her and the animal she was riding.

Then she realised that Harry was already engaged in the age-old battle between man and beast. He was certainly as good a horseman as she had imagined he would be, but even so it took him a little time to get his horse under control.

They set off into the Park with Teresa's mount still bucking to show his independence. It was an hour later, when they were some distance from the Palace that Harry said, "I congratulate you! I have never met or seen a woman who can ride as well as you do."

"Thank you kindly, Sir!" Teresa said in mock humility.

"No, I mean it," Harry insisted. "How can you control that troublesome horse you are riding and at the same time look as if you could be blown away on a puff of wind?"

"That is very poetical," Teresa said. "As I have told my father often enough, I may have my mother's looks, but I inherited his brain as well as his determination." She gave a sigh. "It is a tragedy I was not a boy, but I am fighting with all my strength to persuade my father to let me help him in his business."

"Do you really mean that?" Harry asked in astonishment. "I have never thought that any woman, especially one as pretty as you, would be interested in business."

"I know a great deal about ships and their voyages," Teresa said, "and I intend to learn a great deal more. I find it absolutely fascinating!"

"Now, tell my why," Harry asked. "Quite frankly, I do not think that sort of work is suitable for a woman."

Then they were arguing and fighting each other all the way back to the Palace. Teresa thought as she went upstairs to rest that she had "held her own". She was also certain that Harry was convinced that in many ways she was right.

When she was dressed she went downstairs, anxious to see more of the Palace. All four went from room to room, the Marquess thrilled to show them his possessions. At the same time, he made it absolutely clear that the reason why the Palace looked as splendid as it did now was entirely due to Sir Hubert.

When they sat down to dinner it was Teresa who changed the conversation. She wanted to discuss the Racecourse and the jumps her father had erected on it. Sir Hubert said how high they were, and Harry exclaimed, "I think they will be far too high for any woman, and therefore to-morrow we had better have a flat race."

Sir Hubert smiled. "I thought you realised this afternoon," he said, "when you went riding with my daughter, that Teresa is a 'chip off the old block', and I have never yet found a jump that could defeat me."

"I really think . ." Harry began. Then he saw that Teresa was laughing at him.

"All right, you win!" he said. "But if you have a nasty fall, it is your responsibility, so do not blame me!"

"I shall only blame myself," Teresa said, "and you will have to admit sooner or later that a man is not as superior as he likes to believe."

"The whole trouble is women!" Harry retorted. "They will intrude on what is essentially a man's province. Before we know where we are, we will have women jockeys, and doubtless women as soldiers and sailors!"

He laughed at this, and Teresa said, "Stranger things have happened, and I think the truth is that as a male you are afraid that if we have the chance, we will show you that we are not only your equal, but your superior."

The three men all laughed at this, but Teresa went on, "We shall have to wait and see, but I am sure that one day you will find that women can rule the world, just as well as men."

"They have done it for thousands of years from the pillow," the Marquess retorted, "and that is as far as it should go."

They were still arguing and finding it very amusing when Sir Hubert suggested they should all go to bed. As he walked up the stairs beside Teresa he said in a voice which only she could hear, "You have been wonderful, my dearest."

She kissed her father a fond good-night. When she reached her Bedroom she was thinking that it had been one of the most enjoyable days she could ever remember. What was more, she liked Harry.

She could understand the Marquess's horror at the idea of him marrying an actress with whom, actually, he would have very little in common.

She knew now that all the complimentary things that had been said about him by the Duke of Wellington were true. He would be a good commander of men and use his brain as well as his rifle in fighting the enemy. Now he should be in a position, she thought, to help the country during the peace.

It would be a waste for him to spend his evenings watching his wife perform on a stage. He should put his knowledge to use in amending and improving the Laws of England in the Houses of

Parlimaent. Then, because she was tired, Teresa slept peacefully.

When morning came, Teresa rose early to go riding with Harry before breakfast. Her father had said he wished to conserve his energy for the race that would take place in the afternoon.

Teresa and Harry set off in the sunshine. It seemed to her that everything was enchanted. There were the golden Spring flowers under the trees and birds singing among the green leaves.

She turned back to look at the Palace. It was an attractive background increasing her joy of the horse she was riding. And there was the excitement, and she admitted to herself that it was an excitement, of arguing with Harry.

When they returned for breakfast she felt they had fought a duel with words. While no one had been the winner, they were both proud of what they had achieved. The rest of the day was very exciting.

To Teresa's delight her father won the Steeple chase over the jumps by a head. She had to admit that both men were faster than she was, but she was only half a length behind them.

Sir Hubert was very pleased with himself, and Harry congratulated him. "You have beaten me, Sir Hubert," he said.

There was just a touch of surprise in his voice. "Shall I say it is due to having a little more experience, my boy, and that is something you need in everything you do, whether you are riding, running a business, or planning an offensive against an enemy."

"That is true," Harry admitted, "and of course, I can understand now where your daughter gets her expertise as well as her brains."

"That is the sort of compliment I like," Sir Hubert smiled.

"I only wish I had beaten you both," Teresa said, "but I will manage it another day – you wait and see!"

They laughed at the determination in her voice and teased her all the way back to the house.

It was only when she went up to dress for dinner that Teresa suddenly remembered what was to happen to-night.

It was the Marquess who had said to her father, "Things are going so well between the young people that I wish we dare wait for another day, but after what Charles Graham said, I am frightened that Harry will go back to London tomorrow."

"I thought of that," Sir Hubert replied. "I therefore arranged before I left London," the Marquess went on, "for an actor to arrive tomorrow to play the part of the Priest. I have promised him a lot of money for doing so, and of course arranged one of my own carriages to bring him down."

"If he is an actor, it would be a mistake for Harry to see him," Sir Hubert said. "It would be a disaster if he recognised him."

"I think that is very unlikely," the Marquess replied, "and it was not easy to get a man I could trust not to talk about it. I made it a condition for which I have paid heavily."

Sir Hubert sighed. "It is so delightful being here. I wish we did not have to do this."

The Marquess looked round the room in which they were sitting. "Can you imagine this house and estate being run by a woman whose only claim to fame is that she looks attractive behind the footlights?"

"Camille Clyde is, I believe, a good actress," Sir Hubert remarked.

"Mouthing words, like a parrot, that have been written by somebody very much more intelligent than she is ever likely to be!" the Marquess said savagely.

"You are right – of course you are right," Sir Hubert agreed, "and as you say, we have to save him, so I suppose this is the only way."

"I cannot think of any better," the Marquess said, "and by this time on Monday, it might be too late."

"Yes, of course," Sir Hubert sighed.

Teresa was dressed for dinner when her father knocked on the door. As the maid opened it he said, "I thought you would be ready, my dearest, and I wanted to speak to you alone."

The maid, who had been helping Teresa, quickly went from the room and shut the door behind her.

"What . . has happened?" Teresa asked a little nervously.

"Nothing, so far," her father replied, "but as I told you, the Marquess has an actor who will perform the

Marriage Service, and he has taken care to be correct in every detail."

Teresa was listening, and her father went on, "He has even taken out a Marriage Licence which you know is essential for a marriage to be legal."

Teresa knew all this was essential. When he learned he had been tricked, Harry might insist that the marriage was illegal. He could even go so far as to threaten to take it before the Courts. If this happened, the Marquess would have to explain that it was in fact only a fake marriage. And as it would be talked about there would undoubtedly be a scandal.

As if her father was following her thoughts, Sir Hubert said, "What we have to make sure, my dearest, and I am so sorry you have to do this, is that Harry believes it to be completely and absolutely legal."

He added somewhat tentatively, "He may be angry at being deceived, although there will be no point in him speaking of it to Camille Clyde." He paused before going on slowly, "In fact, if I am not mistaken, he will accept the situation, and when we are quite sure that he is no longer infatuated with the woman and prepared to forget her, we can tell him the truth."

"You .. do not .. think," Teresa said hesitatingly, "that if you .. talked to him .. Papa, and told him .. how much it was .. upsetting Uncle Maurice .. he would give her .. up of his .. own free .. will?"

Sir Hubert thought for a moment. "He might do," he said. "But he might also say angrily that we were interfering in his private life. In which case he would go straight to London and marry her, if only to prove himself to be man enough to decide his own future without any interference."

Teresa knew this was a distinct possibility. She was well aware, having been with Harry ever since they arrived, that he was a strong and determined man. He might be young, but she thought that in some way he was like her father.

Once he had made up his mind, it would be very difficult to make him change it. With a little sigh she said, "I am sure . . you are . . right, Papa, and we . . must therefore . . go ahead . . but I do not . . like it!"

"Nor do I, my dearest one," Sir Hubert agreed, "but we could not refuse to help the Marquess in what is undoubtedly his darkest hour."

"No, of course not," Teresa replied. "He loves Harry and he loves this magnificent Palace."

"And I love you, my precious daughter!" Sir Hubert replied. "I would not have you involved in this if I did not know that it would crucify the Marquess if he thought everything he had worked and strived for these past years was to be wasted on a common woman who would not appreciate it."

"Why cannot Harry see that?" Teresa asked.

"Men are strange creatures," her father answered, "and however strong they may seem to be, a clever woman can twist them round her little finger, and make them do things which later makes them ashamed and sorry."

He was looking at his daughter as he spoke. He thought it almost incredible that any man, especially one who had been away from England for so long, should not fall in love with Teresa as soon as he saw her. It was not only her beautiful features, her large eyes and the pale gold of her hair. There was something else which Sir Hubert recognised was unique about her.

It was something he knew would be irresistibly attractive to the young gentlemen she would meet in the *Beau Monde*.

"No one must ever know of this," he said in a harsh tone. "It would be disastrous for your reputation that you should be mixed up in anything so sordid."

Teresa put her hand over her father's. "Do not worry, Papa," she said. "I am sure that when Harry wakes up to reality he will realise, if nothing else, whatever you and Uncle Maurice have done, it is because you love him."

Then she added rather unexpectedly, "I am sure he misses his mother, and although Uncle Maurice has been wonderful to him, it cannot be quite the same as having your own parents, as I have you."

Sir Hubert was very touched by his daughter's words. He bent and kissed her on the cheek. "I expect the actor has arrived by now," he said, "and when he does come, we will get the Service over. Then we will no longer have to go on talking and arguing about it."

The way her father spoke made Teresa aware of how much he disliked having to deceive a young man of whom he was very fond. But like the Marquess, he could think of no other way of preventing a marriage which would undoubtedly be a failure. Then Harry's future would be ruined.

When her father left her, Teresa took a last look at herself in the mirror. She was wearing a white gown. It had been bought by the Countess for her to wear at one of the Balls to which she would be invited.

It was made of soft white muslin, and was exquisitely embroidered on the breast and round the hem with small silk flowers.

They were decorated with diamantés which glittered, and there were silver ribbons also glittering which crossed over the front and cascaded down the back almost to the floor.

The diamantés shimmered with every move Teresa made. On her head was a wreath of the same silk roses, also glittering with diamantés. She looked very young and very lovely.

She might have been the Goddess of Spring, stepping into the world at the rising of the sun. As she went down the stairs, Teresa wondered if Harry would admire her. Then some cynical part of her brain told her that he would be thinking of someone with red hair.

An actress waiting for him in London.

In the Drawing Room she was aware that Sir Hubert asked the Marquess a question she could not hear.

He did not reply, but shook his head.

It made her think that the actor they were expecting

had not yet arrived, and to them it might seem a disaster.

Teresa had a sudden hope that she would be able to ride with Harry tomorrow morning.

She prayed that he would not be very angry that she had taken part in tricking him!

"Oh . . why . . why do I have to do . . this?" Teresa asked despairingly as they moved into the Dining Room.

# CHAPTER FIVE

Dinner was nearly finished.

They were laughing at a joke made by Sir Hubert when the Butler came to the side of the Marquess, and handed His Lordship a note.

The Marquess read it and nodded his head.

Teresa guessed he was saying that the actor had arrived, and she felt her heart give a little throb.

She knew she was right when a few minutes later the Marquess said, "Before we return to the Drawing Room, I have a special treat for you all."

"What is that?" Sir Hubert asked.

"His Majesty gave me a bottle of his special Port just before I was leaving London," the Marquess answered. "He says it is the best he has ever drunk. We have to taste it and tell His Majesty whether he is right or wrong."

They all laughed at that because the King never

admitted he was wrong in any circumstances.

The Marquess went to the sideboard on which there was a decanter of Port. He poured out four glasses. Teresa guessed that he put two drops of the drug into Harry's glass. The Marquess then carried them to the table.

He set a glass down in front of each of the three people waiting for them. "Now, what shall be our toast?" he asked.

"I think it ought not to be to a person," Teresa said, "but to the Palace. I know many toasts that have been drunk to it every year, and each time Uncle Maurice makes it more beautiful than the year before."

The Marquess raised his glass. "To Stoke Palace!" he said, "and no heel-taps."

He had given Teresa very little Port of which she took just a sip.

She noticed that her father and Harry drank all that was in their glasses. She could not help feeling as if there was a sudden silence. Not only they, but the house itself, were waiting to see what would happen.

With an effort the Marquess went on talking about the Palace, and what further improvements had begun in the garden until his voice died away.

Both Sir Hubert and Teresa realised that the drug had worked on Harry.

He was sitting straight up in his chair as he had done throughout the meal, but now there was a slightly vacant expression in his eyes. He was staring ahead of him and not looking at his Uncle, who was talking and laughing at his jokes.

In a voice that trembled, the Marquess said, "Get up, Harry!"

Obediently, Harry did as he was told.

The Marquess then said in a voice that did not sound like his own, "Let us go to the Chapel and get it over."

Sir Hubert reached out to take Teresa's hand and they walked slowly towards the door.

"Follow them, Harry," the Marquess ordered.

To Teresa, it was frightening to feel that he was just behind her. But he was unaware that she or anyone else was there, or what they were doing.

They walked down the long passage which led to the Chapel which was at the far end of the wing. This also had been designed by Vanbrugh, and Teresa had only had a glimpse of it when they were going round the Palace. Now as she entered it with her father, she was aware that there were flowers on the altar.

The Priest, a man in a white surplice, was standing waiting for them in front of it.

The Marquess, following behind them, realised this was the man the actor had sent him because he could not come himself.

Sir Hubert drew Teresa towards the steps and they waited there until the Marquess and Harry joined them.

Then the Service began.

The Parson was a middle-aged man with his hair just beginning to go grey. He had, Teresa thought, an uninteresting face, and she wondered what parts he played on the stage. He had practically learnt the

Marriage Service by heart. He hurried through it, seldom looking down at the Prayer Book which he held in his hand. Then he came to the responses.

The Marquess, who was acting as Best Man, prompted Harry.

Then when the Priest said: "Now repeat after me . ." Harry did so obediently.

Teresa knew it was foolish of her but she felt very nervous as she said, "*I, Teresa Mary Elizabeth, take thee, Edward Alexander to my wedded husband, to have and to hold from this day forward, in sickness and in health, for richer for poorer, for better, for worse and forsaking all other until death do us part, and thereto I give thee my troth.*"

Harry was handed a wedding-ring by the Marquess which he placed on Teresa's finger. It was, she thought, a surprisingly good fit, and she suspected that it had belonged to his mother.

When the Priest had joined them as man and wife, they knelt for the Blessing.

It was then that Teresa felt ashamed and embarrassed that they were evoking the blessing of the Almighty on what was in fact a lie.

"Forgive us, God," she prayed. "Forgive us for . . acting this farce in a . . sacred place and please . . when he . . learns of it, let Harry . . forgive us . . too."

It was a prayer that came from her heart.

They rose to their feet and on the Marquess's instructions went to a table in the Chancel. The Marriage Register was open for them to sign, Teresa saw lying there the Special Marriage Licence the Marquess had obtained.

As she and Harry signed their names she did not want to think that this was yet another lie. It was wrong, but it was something Harry had to see to convince him that their marriage was legal.

She was glad when the Marquess said, "Now, Harry, give your arm to Teresa and lead her down the aisle and out of the Chapel."

Stiffly, the way he had moved ever since he had been drugged, Harry held out his arm, still looking straight ahead.

Teresa slipped her fingers just inside it and they walked down the aisle together.

When they reached the door the Marquess said in a commanding voice "Now take Teresa into the study."

Harry turned and did exactly as he was told, Teresa moving silently beside him. It was some way to the Study. This was an exceedingly attractive room, which the Marquess had made his own.

It was then Sir Hubert took over. He went to his daughter's side and took her arm away from Harry's. "Go to bed, my darling," he said. "We will tell you tomorrow what has happened. There is no point in you staying here."

"Y . . You are . . going to tell him . . that he is . . m . . married?" Teresa stammered.

Her father nodded. When she hesitated, he took her to the door, opened it and put her outside into the passage. "Go to bed," he said, and it was a command.

Because she had always obeyed her father, Teresa did as she was told. However, she thought it was wrong of her not to stand beside Harry when he received the shock of learning that he was married.

A maid was waiting for her in her Bedroom and undid her gown. Teresa slipped into the large canopied bed. The maid blew out most of the candles, then left the room. There were two candles beside the bed and Teresa lay back against the pillows, wondering what was happening downstairs.

She could guess how horrified Harry would be when they told him what they had done. At the same time, in order to justify herself, she kept repeating over and over again, "It was the .. only way that .. Papa and Uncle Maurice could .. save him."

It was a long time before finally she blew out the last two candles and lay completely in the dark.

Even then as she tried to go to sleep the words "Save him, save him!" were repeating and repeating themselves in her mind.

Teresa awoke because a maid was pulling back the curtains. It was morning, and the sunlight was pouring through the windows creating a golden haze.

The maid came to her bedside. "'Scuse me, Miss," she said, "but 'Is Lordship asks if you'll be downstairs in an hour, as 'e's takin' you away."

Teresa stared at her thinking she could not have heard aright. Then she asked, "You said 'His Lordship'. Do you mean the Marquess?"

"Ow no, Miss," the maid replied. "I means 'Master

'Arry', as they calls him downstairs. 'E's up already, an' says I'm to pack your trunk as you'll be takin' it with you."

Teresa's head was in a whirl, but she thought it a mistake to question the maid any further. She got out of bed and started to dress.

When she was nearly ready the maid came in carrying her breakfast. "I 'opes, Miss," she said, "I've packed everythin' you'll be wantin'."

"Will you go to my father's room," Teresa said, "and tell him I want to see him immediately."

"I'll do that, Miss."

The maid disappeared and Teresa began to eat her breakfast, wondering frantically what had happened.

A few minutes later Sir Hubert came into the Bedroom. "Papa .. what is happening?" Teresa asked. "I have been told that Harry is taking me away."

Sir Hubert shut the door behind him. "I did not know he intended to leave so early," he said, "otherwise I would have come to you sooner."

"Tell me, Papa, what all this is about," Teresa pleaded.

Sir Hubert sat down in a chair. "We waited for nearly two hours last night," he began, "before Harry recovered from the drug. At first he seemed dazed, but then he said, 'I have a headache. Why am I in here?'"

"Then. Then you .. told him?" Teresa asked.

"The Marquess told him that to save him from marrying a woman whom he would never accept at the Palace, he had been married to you. He produced the papers to prove it."

Teresa drew in her breath. "And .. what did .. Harry s .. say?" she asked.

"At first he seemed stunned," Sir Hubert replied, "and I think he was still under the influence of the drug. Then he said, 'You might have trusted me.'"

"I felt sure that is what he would say," Teresa explained, "and he was hurt that Uncle Maurice had not done so."

"We both tried to explain why, if we had not interfered," Sir Hubert said, "he would have married Camille Clyde."

"Did he .. s .. say that was .. what he .. might have done?" Teresa asked.

"He listened to what we had to tell him," her father replied. "Then he went towards the door.

"'I shall leave here tomorrow morning,' he said, in a voice I have never heard him use before."

"'Where are you going?' the Marquess asked."

"'To my own house, where I belong,' Harry replied."

Sir Hubert sighed before he finished, "And that, my dearest, is where you will be going now."

"But .. where is it? .. Do I have to .. go with him?" Teresa asked in a frightened voice.

"Bourne Hall, which is where Harry's family lived, is only about six miles from here," Sir Hubert answered, "and I think, my beloved daughter, you must be brave and accompany him, as he wishes you to do."

He thought Teresa was going to protest, and he added quickly, "I am half afraid Harry might, because he is angry, do something stupid, and what is more important than anything else, is that this is not talked about by anybody, or is written about in the newspapers."

Teresa realised what a mistake that would be and she said, "If you want me to . . go with Harry, I will do so, Papa . . but it is rather . . f . . frightening."

"I know it is, my darling," her father replied, "but I think when Harry realises what we have done was only to help him, he will bring you back here. It was impossible for either his Uncle or I to talk to him last night."

He paused for a moment before he went on, "And to make sure we did nothing of the sort, he locked himself in his Bedroom."

Without speaking Teresa rose and walked to the window. She stood looking out at the Park bathed in sunshine.

After some minutes her father said, "I know we are asking a great deal of you, but, as you are well aware, one's plans, if they are important enough, seldom run as smoothly as one hopes."

"What you are saying, Papa," Teresa said after a moment's silence, "is that I asked you that I might work with you, and this is the opportunity to prove my ability to do so."

"I had not thought of it quite like that," Sir Hubert answered, "but it is in fact, if you wish to put it that way, a test of your ability."

"Then I can only hope I am successful," Teresa said, "just as you would be, if you were in my position." She turned and, picking up the hat which matched her gown, put it on her head.

As her father watched her there was a knock on the door and the maid came in. "I've packed your things in the trunk, Miss," she said. "Can I put your brushes an' combs in your other case?"

"Yes . . of course," Teresa replied.

She looked up at her father who rose to walk to the *boudoir* which was next to her Bedroom. When they were alone again he said, "You are very, very brave, my darling, and I am extremely proud of you. But there is something I have to say to which you must listen carefully."

"I am listening, Papa."

Sir Hubert was finding it hard to choose his words. Then he said, "If by any chance, Harry attempts to take advantage of the fact that he believes himself to be your husband, you must then of course tell him the truth."

For a moment Teresa did not quite understand what her father was implying.

Then as the realisation of it dawned on her, she blushed before she answered.

"I . . I am quite certain . . Papa that if . . Harry is angry with you and . . Uncle Maurice . . he will be . . equally annoyed with . . me."

"In a few days," Sir Hubert said hastily, "I feel sure we will be able to tell him that the whole thing was a hoax."

"B . . But . . supposing," Teresa said in a small voice, "he then . . decides . . to go . . straight to London and . . marry Camille Clyde?"

"The Marquess has thought of that," Sir Hubert replied, "and he will be keeping a close watch on the actress to find out what her feelings are in the matter, or if she is still pursuing Harry."

He put his hand on Teresa's shoulder and drew her a little closer to him as he said, "I know this is asking a great deal of you, but try to keep things going until we are certain that Harry is 'out of the wood'."

"I will try . . Papa, I really . . will try," Teresa promised.

Sir Hubert kissed her and he said, "I am very, very proud of you, and you are behaving exactly as I would want my daughter to behave in an emergency, whatever it might be."

It was only a little later that Teresa walked down the stairs. Her father might think she was brave, but if she was truthful she knew she was very frightened.

The servants had informed her that His Lordship was waiting for her in a phaeton. As they reached the front door she could see him outside. With his tall hat a little to one side of his head, he was sitting upright in the driving seat. There was a Groom behind, and the other side of the open cover of the phaeton was not raised.

"I told Harry to take my phaeton," Sir Hubert said beside Teresa, "because his Uncle requires it." He lowered his voice as he added, "The Marquess intends to go to London either today or tomorrow to find out what that woman is doing."

There was no sign of the Marquess. Teresa kissed her father goodbye and went down the steps, followed by *Rufus*. He had slept on her bed, as he always did, and followed her from there into the *boudoir*. He was now scampering in the delight at being out in the open.

A footman assisted Teresa up onto the high seat beside Harry. *Rufus* jumped up after her and she settled him beside her. She felt he was some kind of protection against Harry's anger.

Without even turning his head in the direction of the front door, Harry drove off. Teresa waved to her father who waved back as they went down the drive. She guessed that while they had been in the *boudoir*, her luggage and Harry's had gone ahead. A brake was usually reserved for the servants, and she was sure Harry's Valet would be in it.

She had an idea that Harry's home, Bourne Hall, had been closed during the war. She could, however, not be certain and did not like to ask questions, so they drove in complete silence.

Harry was tooling the reins with an expertise which she had only seen when her father was driving. The horses pulling the phaeton were a perfectly matched pair of chestnuts. Teresa had an idea that her father had contributed them to the Marquess's stable.

They drove on and on. Teresa was longing to speak to Harry. Even if he abused her it was better than a stony silence. When she glanced at him from under her eye-lashes, she saw that his lips were set in a hard line, and his chin was very square.

She told herself that he was very, very angry, and felt a little quiver of fear run through her.

The sun was shining and it was growing hotter when finally she thought they must be getting nearer to Bourne Hall. They had moved off the main highway into a narrow lane and were forced to slow their pace. The lane twisted and turned and could obviously be dangerous if the horses moved at speed.

They passed a wood on the other side of the lane which made a welcome shade from the heat of the sun. Then they came suddenly to a clearing. There were no hedges, but a copse on the other side of it.

Harry was moving his horses slowly. Teresa guessed that if he could have his way he would have travelled faster. Then from behind some trees a horseman came riding towards them. Teresa glanced at him, then she gave a little gasp.

He was wearing a mask, and had a pistol in his hand. There was another in the sash around his waist. He rode his horse straight into the middle of the road and Harry was forced to pull his team to a standstill.

"Stand an' deliver!" the rider commanded in a thick voice with a coarse accent, "an' Oi'll take ye 'orses fer a start!"

Harry put out his right hand towards the pistol which was in the pocket beside him.

As he moved the Highwayman fired. He aimed at Harry's chest, but, because he was bending sideways, the bullet hit him in the arm.

Teresa gave a shriek and the horses started at the

sound of the pistol shot. It did not, however, disturb the Highwayman's horse.

Then *Rufus* barked. The Highwayman had to hold in his horse, which reared, while Teresa saw he was grasping for the other pistol in his sash.

She knew it was to shoot at Harry again, but, before he got hold of it, she put her arm behind *Rufus*. She snatched the second pistol which her father had told her was in the other pocket.

Without thinking, and with a swiftness that the Highwayman did not anticipate, she shot him in the chest. He gave a shrill cry and fell backwards in the saddle.

As he did so, the Groom behind them jumped down from his seat and climbed up beside Harry. "Oi'll drive, My Lord," he said.

As if he had been wondering how he could manage, Harry moved towards Teresa. He was holding his hand over his arm where the bullet had entered it. "Drive on!" he ordered.

Teresa had a last glimpse of the Highwayman's horse galloping between the trees. His Master had fallen backwards on the saddle, kept there only because his feet were in the stirrups.

The Groom obeyed Harry, moving the horses as quickly as he could along the lane ahead.

Teresa put her arm around Harry's shoulder to support him and his injured arm. He rested against her and he did not speak. She knew he was in pain and although she tried to keep him upright it was difficult.

As if she had asked the question he said after a moment, "I am – all right – and we have not – far to go now – only about two miles."

The lane opened out onto a better road and the horses were able to move at a faster pace.

Teresa tightened her arm around Harry as she realise he was slipping down lower in the seat. Blood was trickling over his hand. "You would not like to stop?" she asked.

"No – get me – home!" he managed to say with what she knew was an effort.

They moved on, increasing their speed until with a leap of her heart Teresa saw some large gates ahead of her. The Groom turned in at them and they were moving up a drive, at the end of which there was an attractive red-brick house that Teresa thought was Elizabethan.

As they drew nearer she could see that she was right. There were diamond-paned windows and the house itself was built in the shape of an "E".

By this time, the blood on Harry's hand had increased and was running onto the rug which covered Teresa's gown.

At last the front door came in sight. As the horses came to a standstill she saw with relief there were two men waiting for them. One of them was Harry's Valet. The Groom brought the horses to a standstill.

Just for a moment, the two men waiting for them stared in astonishment. It was then that Banks, Harry's Valet, came running down the steps.

"There has been an accident," Teresa said. "You

will have to help his Lordship out, but be careful of his arm."

"I'll see t'it, M'Lady," Banks replied.

The way he had addressed her told Teresa that the news of their marriage would have already reached Bourne Hall.

It was with some difficulty that Banks and the other man, who had white hair, lifted Harry out of the phaeton. They were almost carrying him up the steps into the house. Teresa was about to join them when an old man appeared who went to the horses's heads. It was then the Groom said, "I'd best see to 'Is Lordship." He jumped down and ran after the two men who were carrying him.

Carefully Teresa reached the ground with *Rufus* following her.

She could not help thinking that it was *Rufus* who was the hero of the occasion. If he had not barked and frightened his horse, the Highwayman might have fired a second bullet at Harry, which could have killed him.

The mere thought of it made Teresa give a frightened shiver.

She walked up the steps and into the hall.

Now she knew that she was glad – more glad than she could put into words – that Harry was alive!

# CHAPTER SIX

When Teresa walked into the hall she realised it look very unlived in. Through an open door she could see into what she thought was the Drawing Room. All the furniture was covered in Hollands and the blinds were half-drawn.

She started to go upstairs to follow Harry, who was now out of sight. When she reached the landing, an elderly woman came hurrying towards her. She curtsied saying, "I've just heard, M'Lady, that you're married to His Lordship. I wish you both all the happiness in the world – but is he hurt?"

"He has been shot in the arm," Teresa explained.

The woman gave a cry of horror before she said, "I must see him at once! I should explain, M'Lady, I'm His Lordship's Nanny, but I've retired to a cottage in the grounds."

"Then I am sure, Nanny, you are the one person

we want at this moment," Teresa said. "I am trying to find out how to send for the Doctor."

"Mr. Dawson'll see to that," Nanny answered. "I'll tell him you want him," and she hurried away towards the room at the end of the passage.

She felt that, with Banks and Nanny tending to Harry, there would be nothing for her to do. It would be best for her to concentrate on sending for the Doctor.

She stood hesitating whether to stay upstairs or go down. Then the man with grey hair whom she now knew to be the Butler came hurrying towards her. "Nanny tells me, M'Lady," he said, "that you want to send for th' Doctor."

"I think we should have one immediately," Teresa replied.

"I'll see to it, M'Lady."

He went down the stairs and Teresa followed him. By the time she had reached the hall again he had disappeared. She looked into the Drawing Room, then into a room next to it which she realised was the Library.

She could see that the rooms were very attractive with their diamond-paned windows. All the furniture was covered up, and it was therefore difficult to imagine what the house had been like when Harry's mother and father had lived there.

Dawson came back. "I've sent for th' Doctor, M'Lady," he said. "He lives at th' end of th' village."

"Thank you," Teresa said. "I understand you are the Butler."

"So I was, M'Lady," Dawson replied, "but since his Lordship and her Ladyship was killed, there be only me and Mrs. Dawson to do everything."

Quite suddenly, almost as if her father was guiding her, Teresa knew what she must do.

This was Harry's home.

Because he was angry he had come here like a little boy running for comfort to his mother. He had been injured in the process.

Aloud she said, "You were here at the time his Lordship's parents were alive?"

"I've bin here nigh on thirty years, M'Lady," Dawson said, "but things has bin very dull an' quiet with the house empty."

"Then what we must do now," Teresa said, "is to restore everything to how it was when His Lordship's parents were here." Dawson stared at her and she went on, "I imagine you had some footmen here to help you?"

"Three, M'Lady."

"I am sure there must be young men in the village who are looking for work."

Dawson gave a gasp and she continued, "And if your wife is the cook, she will need two or three women to help her in the Kitchen, and of course a scullion."

She paused for a moment before she added, "As His Lordship's Nanny is here, I am sure she will know how to train housemaids who have not been in service before."

Dawson nodded.

"Then tell her to engage three girls from the village," Teresa said.

Dawson was standing as if mesmerised, but at last he spoke, "I can hardly believe what I'm hearing, M'Lady. It's something I think would never happen again."

There was a break in his voice and Teresa saw there were tears in his eyes. "This is His Lordship's home," Teresa said quietly, "and when he is well enough to come downstairs, he must find it exactly as it was when he was a boy."

It was impossible for Dawson to speak. He hurried away to the Kitchen. Teresa was sure she had just turned his world upside-down.

The Doctor arrived surprisingly quickly and when he had examined Harry he said to Teresa, "I have removed the bullet. Fortunately, it is only a flesh wound, and did not touch the bone."

"That was something I was afraid might have happened," Teresa replied.

"His Lordship has, however, lost a lot of blood," the Doctor went on, "and will undoubtedly run a high temperature. But you can trust Nanny. She has been here ever since I can remember and is better than any Nurse I could recommend."

"Then we are very lucky to have her," Teresa smiled.

"It was quite a shock to learn that His Lordship had married," the Doctor continued, "but I know you will take his mother's place. She was the most charming and lovely person I have ever met."

"Thank you," Teresa said. "I know you will help Harry to get well again quickly."

"It will take time, and he will be in pain," the Doctor said, "so do not be too impatient. I will call in again this evening."

He bowed to Teresa and hurried down the steps to where his chaise was waiting for him. It looked somewhat dilapidated and the horse drawing it was obviously getting on in years. As he drove away Teresa thought that, with this house unoccupied perhaps he had no rich patients in the neighbourhood.

Now that he had gone she decided she could go and see Harry. She felt a little leap of her heart as she ran up the stairs towards the Bedroom.

Harry felt as if he was waking up, and yet at the same time, he was dreaming.

There was somebody talking to him. It was a soft voice he recognised because he had heard it many times before. There was also a cool hand moving gently over his forehead.

"Now you are getting well again," somebody was saying, "you will soon be up and about and see that your home is just as you remember it. The flowers are all coming out in the garden, the birds are singing in the trees, and they will all be thrilled that you are with them again."

Harry was listening and could understand every word that was being said. He thought however that they were words he had heard before and sounded to him like music.

Then the soft voice went on, "The horses are waiting for you in the stable and, as I am finding it very lonely riding without you, please, hurry and get well. There is so much I want to talk to you about."

There was silence and the hand was removed from Harry's forehead. Slowly, with an effort, he opened his eyes. Looking down at him with her face very near to his was someone he thought he knew, someone very lovely.

Then the woman, whoever she was, exclaimed, "You are awake! Oh, Harry, you are awake! Can you hear me?"

"Where – am – I?" Harry managed to murmur.

"You are at home, at Bourne Hall, and Harry, you are better!"

The words sounded excited and like a paean of joy.

Harry tried to understand where he was and what had happened, but he was very tired. He shut his eyes.

The hand was back on his forehead again and he thought it must be his mother taking care of him.

Dr. Stuart came down the stairs to find Teresa waiting for him in the hall. "What is the verdict, Doctor?" she asked.

"You know as well as I do that Your Ladyship and Nanny have worked miracles!" he replied. "I have never known a wound to heal so quickly, and now, of course, His Lordship is agitating to get up!"

"May he do that?"

"Tomorrow, but only for a short while," the Doctor insisted. "And he is not to ride until the end of the week."

"You know that is what he is longing to do," Teresa said. "I have to take the horses in rotation to make sure they each have enough exercise."

"I hear you have enlarged the staff in the stables," Dr. Stuart said. "Poor old Abbey could never have managed by himself. He is like a new man with all those lads to help him."

"We are going to need more," Teresa said. "I had a letter from my father telling me he has bought Harry two more horses from Tattersall's, and they should be arriving to-day."

"If you go on like this," Dr. Stuart said, "you are going to need a vet as well as a doctor. I like my patients to have two legs, not four!"

Teresa laughed and waved to him as he drove off. Then she hurried upstairs to see Harry.

She had written to Sir Hubert telling him what had occurred on their way here. She had added however that it would be a mistake for either him or the Marquess to come and see Harry. She wrote. ". . *he has been unconscious for three days, and the Doctor says he must be kept very quiet until the wound has healed.*"

She knew she was really giving them an excuse to keep them away. If Harry was still angry at the way he had been tricked into marrying her, it would upset him again to see his Uncle or her father. She was sure they were clever enough to "read between the lines".

When Harry was conscious they had talked of many things, but did not mention their marriage.

Teresa told him how she had engaged more household staff, and that he also had four gardeners. She told him too how she had added to the numbers in the Stable. He did not say that he was pleased at what she had done, nor did he disapprove.

When he was well enough to sit up in bed, she thought he looked even more handsome than when she had been "married" to him. He had lost weight and his skin was a little paler than it had been before. His features had sharpened.

She could not help comparing him to the statue of a Greek God the Marquess had at Stoke Palace.

Nanny was a tower of strength, making Harry obey her, just as she had when he was a small boy. "Come along now," she would say to him, "you will never get well if you don't eat up all your food."

"I am not hungry," Harry would complain.

"Well, you can't send your plate away untouched," Nanny said tartly. "It'll break Mrs. Dawson's heart, when she's half-killing herself to please you!"

Yesterday Harry had eaten far more of his luncheon than he really wished to. Nanny carried off his empty plate in triumph.

Teresa had laughed. "I never thought to see you obeying a woman!" she said, "I know only too well how you feel they should behave – quiet, gentle, subservient, and of course humble."

"I shall expect all those things from you!" Harry

replied. It was the first time he had acknowledged even indirectly that they were married.

Teresa had for the moment felt shy and a little embarrassed. Then Harry said before she could speak, "You talk in a much more gentle way than you did before you came here."

"I have been thinking of you as an invalid," Teresa replied.

"Personally, I think it is a great improvement!" Harry remarked, "and just the way women should talk."

"I think you are deliberately provoking me into an argument," Teresa complained, "and it is unfair because you know as well as I do that the Doctor said you are to be kept quiet and not to worry about anything."

"Do you think that is what I am doing about you?" Harry asked.

"I am not flattering myself in any way," Teresa replied, "but I have the feeling you are longing to have one of those fiery duels we enjoyed when we were . . riding."

She had been about to say "before we were married", but thought it would be a mistake. Since Harry had recovered he had not made any reference to anything that had happened before they came to Bourne Hall. Now as Teresa sat down beside him in the window, the sun coming through the open casement turned her hair to gold.

"I tell you what I would like to do," Harry said.

"What is that?" Teresa asked.

"When I come down tomorrow, I want to see all the new horses that are in the Stable. I will sit on the top step outside the front door, and you can arrange for them to be paraded in front of me."

Teresa clapped her hands. "That is an excellent idea! Old Abbey is longing to show you the new horses, especially the last two. They are superb!"

"I suppose you have been riding them," Harry said.

"How could I resist doing so?" Teresa asked.

There was a little note of anxiety in her voice. He might resent her riding his horses before he could do so himself.

But he merely smiled and said, "Do not wear them out before I have had a chance of riding them."

"I will try not to," Teresa teased, "and of course they are waiting for you, just as the whole Estate is longing to see you, as soon as you are well enough."

Harry looked at her enquiringly, and she said, "I have called on the farmers who are thrilled that you have come home. I hope you will not mind, but I have told them to go ahead with increasing their crops and their livestock." She thought he might be angry and added quickly, "It is essential they should get all the improvements put in hand before the Winter."

Harry was silent for a moment. Then he said "I have an idea that you have changed your direction from your father's shipyard to my Estate."

Teresa looked at him anxiously. "I do hope you do not think I am interfering," she said, "but there is so much that wants doing, and we have to start somewhere."

"You are quite certain that is what I want?" Harry asked.

There was a little silence before Teresa answered. "I thought it would be . . a mistake for you to see the . . house and the . . grounds as they looked when we arrived."

"Why?" Harry asked briefly.

"Because I thought it . . would upset you. After all, this is your home." There was silence again.

Then Teresa said, "I am . . sorry if I have . . encroached on what is your . . prerogative."

"I will tell you whether you are right or wrong," Harry said, after a long pause, "when I leave this room. But from the window I can see that the garden looks as if someone cares for it."

"They have worked so hard," Teresa said, "so that when you come downstairs you will think they have performed a miracle!"

"Or *you* have!"

She was not certain if Harry was accusing or complimenting her. She got up and went to look out of the window. Unexpectedly Harry held out his hand.

"Come here," he said.

She did not move and after a moment he asked, "Have you forgotten so soon your promise to obey me?"

Teresa blushed. She had no wish at the moment to talk about the mock Marriage Service. Slowly she walked towards him and took his hand. He pulled her closer to his chair and said, "You saved my life and you have been kind and compassionate and very much a woman since I have been ill. I am just wondering how I can thank you."

She looked down into his eyes. Suddenly, she felt as if something very strange was happening within her breast. The way Harry was looking at her was very different from the way he had looked at her in the past. She felt a little quiver run through her and her fingers trembled in his.

Now he was pulling her down towards him, and she knew instinctively that he intended to kiss her. It was then she gave a little cry and pulling her hand from his sh e said, "Oh, Harry . . I have . . something to . . tell you . . something . . t.terrible . . but I think you are . . strong enough to . . hear it."

Harry stiffened. "What has happened?" he asked.

Teresa was feeling wildly for words. Because for a moment they would not come to her lips she moved back to the open window.

"What are you trying to tell me?" Harry asked quietly.

"It . . it will . . make you very . . angry," Teresa said, "and . . perhaps I am . . making a . . mistake in telling you now . ."

"If it is something I have to know sooner or later," Harry said, "I am prepared to hear what it is."

There was a sharpness in his voice that had not been there before.

Teresa thought despairingly that she was making a

terrific mistake. She should have waited. Then in a voice he could hardly hear, she said miserably, "It .. it is just .. that you .. have been .. tricked again and .. although it will .. make you angry .. it was only .. done because .. everybody who loves you .. wanted you to be .. h .. happy."

"I do not know what you are talking about," Harry said. "I know I was tricked into marriage. That is why we are both here, but we have not spoken about it until now."

"I know," Teresa said unhappily, "but I .. I think you .. must now .. know the .. truth .. the whole truth."

"Which is?"

Teresa was trembling, and it was difficult for her to force the words to her lips. "When .. Papa and .. Uncle Maurice .. told you that we .. we were .. m .. married," she said, "it was in fact not .. a .. real wedding. The .. the Parson was an .. actor .. and we were married so that you would not .. go to London .. and marry Camille .. Clyde .. the actress .. as you intended."

Harry stared at her before he said, "Do you think it is right to drug me into taking part in a fake marriage? It seems to me to be an appalling way for two grown men to behave. Naturally it makes me very angry!"

"I .. I know," Teresa whispered.

She ran towards him and knelt beside his chair. "Please do not .. be angry," she pleaded. "It was only because .. Uncle Maurice was terrified that you would make .. a mistake which would .. ruin your whole l

. . life." His face stiffened as she pleaded, "You know how much he . . loves you and everything he has done at the . . Palace has been for you. He was . . desperate as to how he could . . save you from . . yourself."

"So what you are telling me now," Harry said slowly, "is that the marriage was performed by an actor and not a Parson!"

"They had . . to make it appear . . correct in every detail," Teresa murmured. "The . . drug might not have worked . . completely, and you could have been . . aware of what was happening."

"And you agreed to take part in this charade!" Harry remarked. "But, why?"

"Because I . . too love you!" Teresa whispered.

The words were out before she could stop them or think of what she was saying. Then as she saw the expression on Harry's face, she realised what she had said. Lowering her head so that all he could see was her golden hair she said quickly, "You . . did so well in the . . war . . you were . . everybody's . . hero. How could I let you . . as your Uncle was sure you were doing . . throw your life away?"

"I find it hard to believe that my Uncle or your father could behave in such a twisted and extraordinary manner!" Harry said. "Why could they not have asked me outright if I was going to marry an actress?"

"They were . . afraid that if . . they tried to . . persuade you not to," Teresa said, "it might make you more . . determined to . . choose your own wife . . and do what you . . wished to do."

"I suppose I can understand their reasoning," Harry admitted. "At the same time, I very much resent being lied to, and what I dislike more than anything else is the fact that they involved you in this absurd plot!"

"I agreed to take part . . because I was . . doing it for . . you," Teresa said.

"You were worried about me?" Harry asked.

"Of course . . I was!" Teresa answered. "You had been so . . magnificent during . . the war and were a . . hero for . . thousands of people. How could you . . ruin all . . that?"

He did not answer and she continued, "You must be honest enough to . . admit that it would have . . spoilt everything, including this . . wonderful . . beautiful house."

She thought it out every night when she went to bed. The house could never be the background for an actress from the theatre. Teresa felt she could almost see Harry's father and mother moving through the room in front of the fireplace. Or in the Drawing Room with its ancient furniture and Aubusson carpet.

They would be talking about their son who was upstairs in the Nursery. Nanny had shown Teresa proudly the rocking horse Harry had ridden and the Fort on which he had played with his lead soldiers.

As if he knew what was passing through Teresa's mind, Harry asked, "Have you put back everything the way it was when my mother was alive?"

"Nanny and Dawson . . have done it . . really,"

Teresa admitted, "and I am just . . praying you will not be . . disappointed."

"You have done all this for me?" Harry asked quietly. "And yet, you were content to let me believe a lie?"

"It was . . really only a . . white lie," Teresa said, "to . . save you from . . making a terrible . . mistake."

"And what is going to happen to you now?" Harry asked. "You tell me we are not really married, but everybody here at Bourne Hall believes you to be my wife!"

"I think . . Papa expects me . . to . . disappear when . . you are . . well enough," Teresa answered. "I will go back to London to be a débutante which I intended to be before . . all this . . happened."

"It seems to me that you have put yourself in a very difficult position," Harry said, "and if it becomes known that you had stayed with me as the Countess of Lanbourne, it will cause a great deal of gossip and scandal."

"Nobody . . need ever . . know," Teresa said quickly. "Nobody has . . called on you . . and nobody, except for . . the servants, have seen me . . and of course Dr. Stuart."

"I am sure he has told his other patients that I am in residence," Harry remarked.

Teresa made a helpless little gesture with her hands. "You are . . trying to . . make more . . difficulties than there are already," she complained. "Perhaps I should . . not have . . told you so soon. But I thought . . now . . you are no . . longer likely to . . rush off to London.

And perhaps . . just perhaps . . you would be . . happy to be here . . where you belong."

There was a pleading note in her voice as she looked up at him.

There was a pause before Harry said slowly, "I think I could be happy here which, as you say, is where I belong – if I was not alone."

# CHAPTER SEVEN

Sir Hubert opened the letter which he knew was from his daughter and read it eagerly.

*"Darling Papa,*

*I am afraid I have made a mess of everything. I told Harry the truth yesterday and he was very surprised.*

*He then said he was prepared to live here, which I have made exactly as it was when his mother and father were alive, if he was not alone.*

*I knew as he said it that he was thinking of Camille Clyde, and that as soon as he is well enough, which should be in two or three days time, he will go to London.*

*I am sorry, so very sorry, and I should have*

*waited longer, but perhaps by some miracle, she may no longer need him.*

*With so much love from your contrite daughter,*

*Teresa."*

Sir Hubert read the letter through a second time. He then walked across Berkeley Square to the Marquess's house.

The Marquess was reading *The Morning Post*, and he looked up with a smile as Sir Hubert entered. "I am afraid I have bad news," Sir Hubert said.

He held out Teresa's letter as he spoke and the Marquess took it from him. He read it, then said, "I have kept away from the theatre and from Charles Graham. I had now better go and find out what has been happening."

He set off for White's Club thinking it extremely likely that Lord Charles would be there.

He was not mistaken. He had, however, no intention of making anyone suspicious of what he and Sir Hubert had been doing. He therefore talked to one or two other people first, and only then crossed the room to where Lord Charles was sitting near the bow window.

"How are you, Charles?" he asked. "Did you have any luck at the races?"

"My horse came in third," Lord Charles replied, "but I have not seen you lately. Where have you been hiding yourself? I thought you must have gone to the country."

"I went down to Stoke Palace for a short while,"

the Marquess explained, "and now I want to hear all the news – if there is any."

"If you are referring to your Nephew," Lord Charles replied, "I have not seen him for some time, but I hear that the sparkling Camille has a new Protector."

The Marquess knew this was exactly what he wanted to hear. "A new Protector?" he enquired. "Who is he?"

"You remember Durham, a rich, rather boring man, but extremely generous when it comes to diamonds for a 'Pretty Lady'."

The Marquess was delighted, but he tried not to show it. Instead, he merely went from White's to the Garrick Club, where he knew he would find a number of actors and actresses. As soon as he entered he saw the actor he had hired to perform the fake marriage between Harry and Teresa. He walked towards him.

"It is nice to see you again," he said, "and I want to thank you for arranging that little matter we discussed when we last met."

The actor smiled at him. "I hear everything went off well. But I was worried when I could not myself do what you asked. I knew I must find someone else to play the part but it was not easy. Luckily I ran into the Reverend Barton who, as I expect you know, is the Vicar of the Mayfair Chapel."

The Marquess stared at him. Then in a voice that did not sound like his own, he said, "Are you telling me that Barton performed the Marriage Service for my Nephew in your place?"

"I could not find anyone else who would sound convincing," the actor said, "and at least he knew the Service by heart!"

The Marquess was speechless. He was well aware that the Mayfair Chapel was notorious. The first Vicar who was appointed married anyone who would pay him a guinea without asking questions. He had previously solemnised clandestine marriages in the environs of the Fleet Prison.

His willingness to celebrate marriages without Banns or Licence ensured that he was never short of customers. However the Marriage Act was altered in 1754. It became law that the Banns must be read for three Sundays before the marriage took place and registered in a Banns Book. Otherwise a Special Licence had to be obtained from the Archbishop of Canterbury.

The Mayfair Chapel therefore became more or less respectable. A number of people who lived in the neighbourhood were still married there and the Vicar was known to do almost anything for money. The Marquess, however, had bought a Special Marriage Licence in case Harry asked questions.

Therefore he and Teresa were now legally married.

The Marquess knew that it would be a great mistake for the actor to know there was anything amiss. He merely thanked him once again for his help and hurried back to Berkeley Square.

He went to Sir Hubert's house and burst in upon him telling him with horror what had happened. "I am quite certain," he said brokenly, "that Harry will never forgive me for treating him in what is really an outrageous and appalling manner."

Sir Hubert's first impulse was to go to Bourne Hall. He would tell Harry what had happened, and how desperately upset his Uncle was. Then he remembered how Harry had behaved before when he had been told a wife had been chosen for him!

He thought it might make matters worse. Instead he hurriedly wrote a note to Teresa, and a Groom was told to carry it to Bourne Hall as quickly as he could.

Teresa cried herself to sleep.

She had done so every night since she had been convinced that Harry intended to marry Camille Clyde. His Uncle and her father had tried to save him and failed. She noticed unhappily that he never seemed to look at her. She knew he watched her at first when he recovered from his high temperature. Now whenever she talked to him he seemed to be at a distance, or be thinking about something else.

"He is longing to be rid of me," she thought, "and once he has left for London I do not suppose he will ever want to see me again."

She knew as she tossed and turned in her bed that she loved him more and more every day. When he had been unconscious, she had talked to him as she massaged his forehead. She had felt he was like a child who had hurt himself and needed a mother's love to make him feel better. Her mother had told her that even when people were completely unconscious, if you talked to them they were aware of it.

"They might not understand exactly what is being said," Lady Bryan had said, "but it makes them feel safe, and encourages them to get well quickly."

Teresa had therefore talked to Harry from the very moment that he lost consciousness because of his high temperature. She knew now that she had fallen deeply and hopelessly in love with him.

"How could I help it?" she asked herself, "when he is so handsome, and also so clever?"

She would go over and over again in her mind what they had said to each other when they went riding. She remembered the arguments they had and the battles they had fought in words.

"He is so clever and just the sort of man England needs at the moment," Teresa thought, "in Parliament, as well as in the social world."

Then she knew that if Harry was in his rightful place she would have no part in it. Once he returned to London it would be Camille Clyde he would want to be with. If she was not available then he would seek out the sophisticated beauties whose luncheons and dinner-parties would be very different from the dull meals Harry would have at home.

"I do not fit anywhere into that picture," Teresa told herself humbly.

Because she loved Harry and because she knew it was hopeless she made a decision. As soon as he had no further use for her she would ask her father to take her to their house in Lancaster. Sir Hubert had closed it up while she was supposed to be enjoying a Season in London.

Teresa knew now she had no wish to go to Balls, or even to be presented at Court. "I will work with Papa and concentrate on his ships," she told herself.

Loving Harry and talking to him would make any other men she met seem dull and boring. Because she loved him, it would be impossible for her even to love any other man in the same way.

"Papa and Uncle Maurice may have saved him from ruining his life," she said to herself a little bitterly, "but they have ruined mine!"

Then she was crying again as she realised she was reaching for a moon which was completely out of reach.

Harry had enjoyed having the horses paraded in front of him.

Teresa had ridden the most obstreperous. It was one which had just arrived from London, and was younger and not so well broken in as the others her father had bought.

The Groom led it in at the end of the parade, which had passed Harry seated, as he had requested, at the top of the steps. Then for some reason known only to himself, the horse objected to what he was being asked to do.

He reared and bucked, and did everything in his power to unseat Teresa. He very nearly succeeded, but somehow she managed to control him. Finally he joined the parade and moved past Harry, while the Grooms cheered involuntarily.

The horses were then taken to the stables and Harry went back to bed. He was very tired.

Nanny helped him undress having shooed everybody else away. "Like all men," she said, "His Lordship's doing too much too soon, and now you can all leave him alone."

Harry was left alone until the next day, when he again insisted on getting up. He was definitely stronger, and insisted on making a tour of the rooms on the ground floor to see how they had been restored as they were in his mother's day.

That night when they went to bed Teresa went over all that they had said and done during the day. Once again she was sure that Harry, when he was well, was thinking of going back to London to marry Camille Clyde.

Although she told herself she was being absurd the tears ran down her cheeks. Finally she fell into a fitful sleep in which she dreamt of Harry. He was going away and although she had begged him to stay he insisted on leaving. She woke with a start and was thankful to find it was only a dream.

"How can I be so . . stupid?" she asked herself.

Then she thought how handsome he looked as he watched the horses. How fascinating it was to talk to him. She wanted to cry again! The room seemed hot. She got out of bed and pulled back the curtains. One of the casement windows was open but she opened another. Then as she looked down into the garden she was aware there was a light in the room downstairs.

It was in the Drawing Room. She remembered she had gone into it after dinner to collect a book she was reading.

She had taken it up to bed with her. "I must have left a candle burning," she told herself and was ashamed at having been so careless.

She had gone in after the servants had retired to their quarters. This meant that the candle would burn all night and it might, although it was unlikely, cause a fire. She put on her dressing gown which was a pretty one of fine blue wool trimmed with lace on the collar and cuffs. It had little pearl buttons down the front which went from the neck to the hem. She did them up and then walked towards the door.

She realised as she reached it that *Rufus* was behind her. She stopped and said, "Wait! Good dog, sit."

She thought if she took him with her he might bark at something in the hall and that would wake Harry.

*Rufus* sat down. As she went out the door he gave a little whine. "I will only be a minute or two," Teresa whispered to him.

There was always a few lights left on in the passages at night so the place was not completely in darkness. As she crossed the hall there was one light near the front door.

She opened the door into the Drawing Room. Then when she had taken a few steps into the room she stood transfixed.

Standing by the fireplace were two strange men who were lifting down the picture from above it.

Teresa made a little sound of horror and they turned to look at her. It was then she realised that the lower part of their faces were covered with pulled up handkerchiefs. All she could see were their eyes.

"What are . . you doing . . here, you . . have no . . right . ." she began.

Then someone behind her pulled a gag over her mouth. She was aware, too late, that there was another man in the room, who tied the gag tightly.

While she was struggling the two men by the mantelpiece put down the picture and came to help. Almost before Teresa could realise what was happening her arms were roped to her sides. Her ankles were tied together, and she was lifted up by two of the men and carried to the sofa.

They threw her down roughly on to it.

The gag they had tied very tightly was hurting her lips, and she stared up at them in terror.

They picked up a beautifully embroidered Chinese shawl which was arranged over the back of the sofa and threw it over her. She was then in darkness and could see nothing. She was helpless, unable to move and unable to make a sound.

"That'll settle her," one of the men said speaking for the first time.

He had a coarse voice, and Teresa knew he did not come from the country.

"Better hurry all th' same," another man said. "Get 'em boxes out o' th' cabinet."

Teresa wanted to scream at what they were doing. She knew the man who had just spoken was referring to a beautiful collection of snuff boxes which were at the other end of the Drawing Room.

She had looked at them tonight when the Holland had been taken off the cabinet. "They were her Ladyship's pride and joy," Dawson had told her. They were also, Teresa knew, very valuable. Some of them had exquisitely painted miniatures on them framed with diamonds and pearls. Others were of enamel that could only have been made by a master hand. Some were very old and the miniatures were of Kings and Queens who had lived several centuries ago.

How could she let them take away anything so valuable?

She was sure Harry loved them because they had been his mother's. "I must save them, I must," she thought and realised again how completely helpless she was.

It was then she remembered she and Harry had been able to read each others thoughts.

When they had been arguing in one of their spirited duel of words he would say, "I know what you are thinking, I can tell you now before you say it, that you are wrong – wrong."

She had laughed. But she had often known what argument Harry was going to confront her with before he put it into words. "If only he was thinking of me," she thought.

Perhaps she could warn him of what was happening in his mother's Drawing Room.

"Wake up. Wake up," she said in her heart, "Save the . . things you love . . come quickly . . you are . . wanted."

She felt almost as if her thoughts were tiny birds she was sending out from her breast. They could fly from the Drawing Room to Harry's room and might wake him up.

She remembered how her father had told her that in India and other parts of the East a native would use his thought far more effectively than any other way of communication. He told her once when he was travelling that one of the porters in charge of his luggage had said he must leave to go home immediately.

"What has happened?" her father asked.

"My father is dying, and will be dead by the morning and I will be needed."

"Is this what you have been told?" her father asked in surprise.

He knew they were a very long distance from where they had started their journey, and where the man's home was situated.

"I hear it in – my mind," the man replied.

Because he thought the porter was imagining things, her father had said the man could not go home at once. He would try and arrange it in two or three days time.

The man had accepted her father's authority. But he shook his head dismally and said, "By then it will be too late."

"And was it too late?" Teresa asked.

"It was indeed," her father replied. "The man's father had died exactly as he had expected, I could only apologise because I had not believed him."

"That was thought transference," Teresa said slowly trying to understand.

"To the natives in India it comes quite naturally," her father told her, "and it is a pity we do not copy them." He smiled before he added, "It would save us a lot of trouble and a great deal of money!"

Teresa thought of this story now and went on sending her thoughts to Harry. She heard however with despair the thieves taking another picture down from the walls.

The one over the fireplace was a Van Dyke and she had admired it everytime she came into the room. The one they were lifting down at the moment was an exceedingly beautiful flowers picture, painted by Ambrosius Bosschaurt. She was certain it would be a terrible loss to Harry.

One of the servants had told her that his mother had loved flowers. She not only filled the house and the greenhouses with them, but collected flower pictures. "Oh save it Harry . . save it! Hear what I am telling you, and even though you are still weak, come downstairs."

He had been tired when he went up after watching the horses. But he had enjoyed a long rest by now and she knew he was getting stronger all the time. It might be only a question of days before he felt he could go back to London and find Camille Clyde!

When she thought of it, it was as if a cold hand was

squeezing her heart. She wanted to cry out at the pain of it. Perhaps she told herself, this might persuade him to stay in the country. His home had been burgled and the room his mother had loved, defaced!

The man who had been collecting the snuff boxes must have joined the others, because she heard him say, "These be worth a pretty penny an' th' sooner us gets 'em out of 'ere an' up t' London, th' better."

"You be right," one of the other men replied, "an' I thinks we'll take that other picture with us, old Isaac'll fancy that one."

The other man chuckled. "There's nothing old Isaac don't fancy if he can turn a pretty penny on it."

"He'll get more than a penny on that one," the other man replied. "Come on."

They were just about to pass where Teresa was lying on the sofa, when suddenly she heard the door open. Her heart leapt as she heard Harry say, "What the hell is going on here?"

She realised the men who were almost opposite the sofa stopped dead. It shot through her mind that perhaps Harry was unarmed and they would treat him as they had treated her.

Then as she wanted to cry out and warm him she heard him say, "Put your hands up above your heads."

It was an order. It was given so sharply that she thought one of the men had been going to draw a revolver from his waist.

Then as she was still trembling because Harry

sounded alone with three men against him, he said, "Tie them up."

As he spoke, to her relief there was the sound of footsteps behind him. Now with a superhuman effort she managed to roll over on one side. The Chinese shawl fell off her face and she could see once more.

In front of her, as she had known, were the two men who had been taking down the pictures. They were standing with their arms above their heads, and the third man, standing a little way from them had one arm up. With the other he was holding a huge sack.

Teresa knew it contained the snuff boxes he had taken from the cabinet. Facing them was Harry just inside the door. Two footmen with rope in their hands were advancing towards the men who had taken down the pictures.

It was then the man with the bag of snuff boxes made a run for the window. It was a large window and the burglars had got it wide open. The man had actually reached it still holding tightly on to his sack.

Harry fired.

The bullet hit the man in his arm, above the elbow. He gave a shriek, dropped the sack and collapsed on the floor holding tightly on to his arm.

As if Harry thought he must take every precaution, he approached the two men who were being tied up by the footmen. He drew from the belt of one man a pistol and from the other a long shiny knife which made Teresa shudder.

As he turned away from the last man, Harry looked

towards the sofa and saw Teresa. For a second he just stared at her.

Then he moved quickly and putting his hand behind her head undid the gag. As it fell off and she made a little sigh of relief he said, "Are you all right, they have not hurt you?"

"No, they only tied me up," Teresa answered, "I was trying .. desperately to tell you what was .. happening and now you .. have come. How could you have .. known that you were .. wanted?"

Harry smiled. "I heard you," he said.

He turned his attention to the men who were by now roped up. Their arms were behind their backs; their wrists tied so that it was impossible for them to move them. The two footmen, their eyes shining with excitement, were waiting for the next order.

"Take these two men," Harry said, "and lock them up in the scullery or any place from which they cannot escape until the law gets here."

He paused and then continued, "Then come back and I will tell you what to do with the wounded man."

He glanced at him as he spoke. He was writhing in agony and the blood was already running over his hand.

"Wake up someone who will go for the Doctor," Harry went on, "and wake Nanny. Tell her she has another invalid on her hands."

"Hers won't be too pleased to have someone like him," one of the footmen replied.

"I know that," Harry agreed, "but we can hardly allow the man, foul as he is, to bleed to death. Put him on the sofa in the servants hall and see he makes as little mess as possible."

The footmen had their orders. They marched the two burglars ahead of them out of the room. Teresa could hear them going down the passage. She knew it was the most exciting thing that had ever happened to either of them, and she was sure they were enjoying every minute of it.

Harry came back to her. He started to undo the rope which was tied at the back. When her hands were free, she moved her fingers so that the blood could come back into them.

"How could this happen to you," he asked, "and what were you doing down here in the middle of the night?"

"I saw from my window there was a . . light from the . . Drawing-Room and I . . thought I must have . . forgotten to blow a candle out."

As Harry did not speak, she went on: "I was so frightened they would go away with the pictures and your mother's collection of snuff boxes before anyone could stop them. How could you come because I prayed you would?"

Harry smiled. "I must admit we should be very grateful to *Rufus*."

Teresa's eyes widened. "You heard him?"

"He was whining as if he thought you were in danger and when he woke me I was certain something was wrong."

"I left him behind so that he would not wake you," Teresa said.

"A good thing too," Harry answered, "otherwise they might have killed him."

Teresa gave a cry of horror and he went on, "Instead of which he was clever enough to wake me and then I knew, I really did know, that you wanted me."

"I was trying thought transference which Papa told me is used so much in India."

"I was convinced that something was wrong; that was why I brought a revolver with me."

"You saved your treasures by doing so," Teresa said.

Harry had undone her ankles and now she put her feet down on the floor. "I was . . very . . very . . frightened," she said, "but now you are . . entitled to another . . medal at least."

"I think that should be yours," Harry said.

Teresa looked at him as he spoke. She felt as if he was saying something to her she did not understand.

Then Nanny suddenly came through the doorway. She was wearing a dressing gown which made her seem a little strange. Her hair was pinned back tidily in a bun. As she came into the room with an angry expression on her face Teresa felt as if she and Harry were both back in the nursery. They had done something which had turned out wrong and they were therefore in trouble.

"Now what is all this, My Lord?" Nanny asked, "and what are you doing out of bed?"

"I am just saving my house from being burgled,

Nanny," Harry replied, "and they might even have taken Miss Teresa with them as well as the pictures."

"I have never known such goings on," Nanny said. "I always believed the house was properly guarded."

"So did I," Harry said.

Then he walked across the room to the man who was groaning on the floor.

"He is one of the burglars I suppose?" Nanny questioned.

"He has all the snuff boxes in that bag," Teresa cried. "Do be careful that they are not broken or damaged in any way."

As if Harry thought this was likely, he walked across the room and picked up the bag. It was heavier than he had anticipated and as he moved it away from the wounded man he staggered.

"Now go straight back to bed, My Lord," Nanny said sharply, "or we shall have you down with a temperature again."

Harry put the bag against the wall where it was unlikely anyone would stumble over it. Then he said meekly, "Very good, Nanny, I have sent someone for the Doctor and I have told the footmen to put this man on the sofa in the servants hall."

"That place is too good for him if you ask me," Nanny replied. "But I suppose we cannot let him die, as he deserves."

The man of whom she was speaking gave a groan. "Help me," he said, "Help me, I'm in pain."

"You'll have to wait your turn," Nanny said as if

he was a child. "You're very fortunate that anyone will take the trouble over the likes of you."

The way she spoke in her sharp tone when anyone behaved badly, made Teresa want to laugh.

Harry's eyes were twinkling. He put his arm around her. "I think you and I had better go back to bed. We can leave everything in Nanny's capable hands, and we must certainly do what we are told."

"Of course we must," Teresa agreed laughingly.

They went out of the Drawing Room.

As they got outside she realised that Harry was swaying a little. "It has been too much for you," she said. "Hold on to me and I will help you upstairs."

"I was going to help you," he said.

"You saved me," Teresa answered, "which is all that matters."

By this time they had reached the bottom of the stairs. She saw Harry grasp the bannister as if it was a lifeline.

"Put your hand on my shoulder," she said, "and stop being proud, you have had a very exhausting day and nothing could be more upsetting than being burgled."

"I think the truth is," Harry said rather breathlessly as he moved up the stairs. "You should be crying on my shoulder and I should be comforting you."

"I can do that when you are feeling stronger," Teresa said, "but at the moment I am not the soft, weak female you want me to be."

Harry gave a chuckle, but she knew it was an effort for him to reach the top of the stairs.

They went down the corridor in silence. As they passed Teresa's door, *Rufus* started barking and scratching. "I shut him in," Harry said weakly, "just in case there were burglars which I suspected and he attacked them."

"I am sure he would have done so if he thought they were hurting me," Teresa answered. "He is a very brave dog."

"And he has a very brave mistress," Harry replied.

By this time they had reached the door of his room. When Teresa opened it she saw there was a candle alight by the bed.

"I expect Nanny will come up to see if we have carried out her orders, "she said. "So you had better hurry into bed."

"And you must do the same," Harry answered. "Thank you for saving the things I value. That is another thing for which I have to be grateful to you."

"We will talk about it tomorrow," Teresa said.

She watched him move a little unsteadily towards the bed. Then she shut the door and ran to her own room.

*Rufus* was almost breaking down the door by this time. She picked him up in her arms and he wriggled with joy that she was back.

"It is all right," she said, "quite all right. You have saved me you clever dog. It was you who woke the Earl and really you who saved the pictures and snuff boxes."

She hugged him then put him down as she took off

her dressing gown. Then as she got into bed he sprang up so that he could lie beside her.

"There is always something happening when one least expects it," Teresa thought, "and Harry heard me when I wanted him to."

She thought as she put her head down on the pillow that it was wonderful. She could get in touch with Harry through her thoughts and he realised it. Then she told herself that he would certainly not be strong enough to go to London for several days after this had happened. Perhaps in a way it was a blessing in disguise.

"Thank You, God . . thank you," she prayed, "for saving the pictures and the snuff boxes. Please make Harry stay in the country . . please . . please."

She was still praying when she fell asleep.

# CHAPTER EIGHT

Two days later Harry came down to luncheon and announced he would take a rest during the afternoon. Then he would have dinner downstairs.

Mrs. Dawson was in a flurry over the idea. She was determined to tempt him with every delicacy he had enjoyed when he was a boy. Because the staff were so delighted, Teresa forced herself to put on one of her prettiest gowns. It was the one which the Countess had chosen for her in which to be presented.

She told herself as she went downstairs that perhaps this was the last time she would dine alone with Harry. She had the feeling that tomorrow he intended to go to London. She did not know why she thought this because he had not said anything, but she just had a feeling he was planning something, and she was sure it concerned Camille Clyde.

She found him waiting for her in the Drawing Room

wearing his evening clothes. She thought no man could look more handsome or more irresistibly attractive. As she walked towards him her heart turned several somersaults.

"This is a very special occasion, Teresa," Harry said.

"Because you are downstairs?" Teresa asked.

"Because I am well," he answered, "and after dinner I will tell you what I am going to do."

Teresa looked at him apprehensively, but did not ask questions.

When Dawson announced that dinner was ready, Harry offered her his arm. In the Dining Room the candles were lit and Dawson had laid out the best gold and silver plate. As the footmen in their smart livery served them Teresa thought that nothing could be more romantic.

If this was really the last time she would ever dine alone with Harry she would always remember every second of it.

He certainly made an effort to be entertaining. He told Teresa amusing stories about the Army of Occupation which made her laugh. When the meal was finished he accepted a small glass of brandy before Dawson and the footmen withdrew.

"I suppose really I should leave you to your brandy, which you are not drinking," Teresa said.

"It will be more comfortable if I bring my brandy with me into the Drawing Room," Harry replied.

They walked together down the corridor.

In the Drawing Room the chandeliers were lit,

shining on everything that had been cleaned and polished.

Teresa was just about to suggest that Harry sat in a high-backed chair by the fireplace when Dawson came hurrying into the room. He was carrying a silver salver in his hand and on it was a letter.

"This 'as just arrived from London, M'Lady," he said, "an' I thinks th' Groom should stay th' night."

Teresa recognised her father's handwriting as she answered, "Yes, of course, but tell the man not to hurry away to-morrow as I may have an answer for him to take back to my father."

"Very good, M'Lady," Dawson replied.

Teresa opened the letter. "I wonder why Papa has sent this by a Groom?" she said. "He usually posts his letters."

Harry made no reply and she read the letter:

*"My Darling Daughter,*

*I have had the greatest difficulty in writing you this letter because I feel you will be as upset as I am.*

*The Marquess went to London yesterday to find out what has happened to Camille Clyde and as that was good news he was at first very pleased.*

*She has a new Protector in the shape of Lord Durham who is old and very rich but very generous where someone like Camille Clyde is concerned.*

*The Marquess however went on to the Garrick Club so that he could thank the actor who played the part of the Priest in the false marriage which took place between you and Harry.*

*He found the young man and then learned to his horror that as the actor could not take the part as he intended he had in fact sent in his place the Reverend from the Mayfair Chapel.*

*I can hardly bear to put this into words to you my dearest, but this means that as the Marquess has taken so much trouble in getting a Special Licence, the marriage which took place between you and Harry when he was drugged, is completely legal and you are therefore, in the eyes of the law, man and wife.*

*I cannot express how sorry I am that this should happen and the Marquess is completely overcome, but there is nothing he can say or do which will be of any help.*

*We can only beg your forgiveness as I hope Harry will forgive us. Our only excuse is that we were doing it for what we believed was for his own good."*

As if she thought she had misunderstood what her father had written, Teresa read the letter through again.

She got to her feet, hardly knowing what she was doing. Instinctively she moved to reach the window feeling she needed air.

"What is it?" Harry asked in concern. "What has upset you?"

Teresa found it almost impossible to speak.

"Tell me!" Harry persisted, and it was a command.

"I . . I do not . . know . . how to tell you," Teresa said. "And . . you will be . . very . . very angry . . even more . . angry than you were . . before."

Harry raised his eyebrows. "I should have thought that was impossible, but tell me what your father has written."

"I . . I . . cannot," Teresa murmured. "Oh . . Harry . . I cannot . . tell you! How could I have . . known . . how could I have . . guessed that . . this would . . h . . happen!"

"Give me the letter!" Harry said.

Because once again he was commanding her, she moved towards him.

He took the letter from her with one hand and held onto her wrist with the other. "I cannot imagine why you should be so upset!" he said.

"Y . . You will . . see why . . when you read what . . Papa has . . written," Teresa answered incoherently.

She was so upset yet she could not pull away from him. Without thinking she crouched down beside his chair. Harry started to read the note, and Teresa laid her head against him.

She was too frightened to see the fury on his face, and hear the anger in his voice. There was silence; a silence that Teresa felt was like a dark cloud that completely encompassed her. Then, unexpectedly, Harry laughed.

It was a choked laugh, as if he could not help himself. Teresa stared up at him in astonishment, and he said, "I have never met such a couple of old muddlers! They should be ashamed of themselves!"

"I . . I am sorry . . so terribly . . s . . sorry," Teresa cried. "I thought . . you would be . . free . . but . ."

"They bungled it!" Harry interrupted. "Really! Two grown men! I never imagined my Uncle or your father could behave so foolishly. It is incredible!"

Because she did not understand, Teresa could only stare at him. Unexpectedly, he put his arm round her.

"I was going to ask you this evening," he said quietly, "if, my darling, you would marry me. However, my Uncle and your father have done that already!"

"Y . . You . . were going to . . ask me to be . . your wife?" Teresa asked breathlessly.

She thought she could not have heard him aright, or that Harry was merely teasing her.

He drew her a little closer. "I love you!" he said. "I have loved you ever since I first saw you."

"I do . . not believe . . it!" Teresa whispered.

"I will make you believe it," Harry promised, "for I think, my darling, that you love me a little."

Teresa hid her face against his shoulder. "I do . . love you," she said brokenly, "but . . I never . . thought . . you could . . ever love . . me."

"How can I help it," Harry answered, "when you saved my life and are everything a man could want in his wife? Also so beautiful that whenever I look at you, I think I must be dreaming."

"How can . . you say such . . things to . . me, Harry, when I have . . been so very . . unhappy thinking . .

you were going back .. to London .. to marry .. someone .. else?" She could not bring herself to say the actress's name.

"I never intended to marry anyone – except you!" Harry said.

Because she was so surprised, Teresa raised her head. "B .. but .. your Uncle .. thought .."

"I know exactly what he thought," Harry interrupted, "and if he had had the sense to ask me instead of drugging me with that Chinese filth, I would have told him I was trying to ask him for his advice as to the best way of getting myself out of a somewhat tricky situation."

Teresa was listening wide-eyed, and he said, "I had better tell you what happened and 'clear the decks' once and for all."

"Yes .. please .. tell," Teresa begged. "I cannot .. imagine how .. all this has .. happened."

"It happened," Harry explained, "because I found Camille Clyde a very amusing person to be with, and after years of being away from London, I wanted to enjoy all the delights that were available."

"I .. can understand .. that," Teresa murmured.

"I thought you would," Harry said, "you are a very understanding, very intelligent person."

He paused for a moment to look down at her as if he wanted to kiss her. Then, as if he felt he must go on, he said, "One night after we had attended a dinner-party and had a great deal too much to drink, Camille said, I thought jokingly, 'I think it would be a good idea if we got married.'"

"Because I was not thinking very clearly, I replied, 'It would be a better idea if you behaved as if you were my wife!'

'I kissed her and after that she used to tease me by saying 'Now kiss me as if I was your wife.'"

He paused for a moment, as if he was looking back. Then he went on, "Quite suddenly I realised that what had been a game was getting serious! I suspect that was when Camille told her friends that we were actually to be married."

He looked down at Teresa and said quietly; "I swear to you, my precious, that the only time I have ever considered putting another woman in my mother's place was when I met you."

"Oh . . Harry . . is that . . really . . true?"

Because it seemed so wonderful, Teresa felt the tears fill her eyes. Now they trickled down her cheeks.

"I swear it is the truth," Harry answered, "and I know, my beautiful darling, that you are exactly the sort of woman my mother would have chosen for me as my wife."

He pulled her closer still and wiped away her tears. Then he was kissing her; kissing her possessively, demandingly, as if he was afraid of losing her. To Teresa it was as if the Heavens opened and Harry carried her inside.

She had never been kissed before. It was a rapture beyond anything she could imagine, or thought she was capable of feeling. Harry kissed her and went on kissing her until they were both breathless.

Then he said, "My darling, my sweet, my wonderful little wife, I know we will be happy."

"I love you . . oh . . how I love . . you!" Teresa whispered.

Harry pulled her closer to him so that they were squeezed together in the big chair.

"I was going to ask you this evening," he said, "if you would marry me."

"I . . I thought you were . . going to . . tell me that you were . . going back to London . . and did not . . want me here any . . more."

"How can you imagine anything so ridiculous?" Harry asked. "I have not dared look at you or touch you until I was well enough to feel I was a man again but, my precious, I have wanted to kiss you ever since I listened to you talking to me and soothing my brow, when I thought at first you were my mother."

Teresa hid her face against his neck. "I thought somehow you were a . . child that had been . . hurt," she whispered, "and I had to make you . . well again."

"That is what you will do to our children," Harry said, "and I know they will all ride as well as we do."

Teresa gave a little laugh.

"You are . . going far too . . fast!" she protested. "I have not . . yet grown . . used to the . . idea that I am . . really married to . . you."

"I have been planning our marriage in my mind," Harry said, "and now we are going to be married again."

"Again?" Teresa queried in astonishment. "How can . . we?"

"Very easily," Harry said. "I had already decided that our marriage must be completely secret because everybody thinks we are married already."

He paused and then continued:

"I know the old Vicar who christened me will be only too pleased to marry us, and then we could trust him never, in any circumstances, to tell anyone what he has done."

"But now we know our . . first marriage was not . . just pretence!" Teresa murmured.

"If you think I want to be married and not even remember the Service, you are very much mistaken!" Harry said.

He smiled and then said, "Especially as I am marrying the most beautiful, the most perfect and the cleverest woman a man could possibly have."

"Oh, Harry . . that is . . what I want . . to be . . for you!"

"So to-morrow evening we will be married here in the Chapel," Harry went on, "and there will be no need for anyone to know what has actually taken place. I shall merely say it is a Service of Thanksgiving for my recovery from being shot."

Teresa gave a cry of joy. "You are so clever," she said, "you think of everything!"

"I think of you," he answered, "and, my darling, you are never going to forget marrying me properly with both of us in full command of our senses and, of course, – our hearts!"

He pulled her to him and kissed her again.

Teresa knew that his love for her was as deep and complete as hers for him. "I love . . you!" she said.

But the words were very inadequate to describe her feelings.

Teresa knew the next morning from the moment Harry came down to luncheon that he was making the day a very special one.

It was their real Wedding Day.

Although Harry wanted to ride he contented himself visiting the stables and admiring the horses. He arranged that he and Teresa would ride the following day.

When they were in the Study, Harry said, "I have decided that when we are not here at Bourne, I should learn how to make money, by working with your father as you wanted to do."

Teresa gave a cry of excitement. "Oh, Harry, that would be marvellous for Papa, and I would love it too!"

"Then that is what we will do," Harry said in a tone of satisfaction.

"We must also spend a lot of time here," Teresa suggested.

"Of course," Harry agreed.

"But . . what about . . Stoke Palace?" Teresa's voice was worried.

"When Uncle Maurice dies," Harry answered, "which will not be for years, we will give Bourne Hall to our eldest son and move into the Palace."

Teresa laughed. "You are going too fast!" she protested.

At the same time, the future could not seem more glamorous or exciting.

Without Nanny pressing him he went to lie down about tea-time and insisted that Teresa do the same. She had the feeling that he had been planning very carefully exactly what would happen.

She thought the way he looked at her with love in his eyes was the most wonderful thing that could possibly occur in the whole world.

She lay in bed thanking God over and over again that she had found love. Now the future was brilliant with sunshine, flowers and everything was beautiful.

"I shall be with Harry, listening to Harry and talking to Harry," she told herself. "Please God, make him go on loving me."

When she got up she learned that they were having an early meal and Harry was coming down for it. She went to her wardrobe and took out the prettiest dress she possessed. She knew it was very becoming, and it made her look very young, and at the same time ethereal. She might have stepped out from under the trees in the wood.

She thought, despite all their arguments together and Harry thinking her too clever, it was what he would want on his Wedding Day.

She looked very feminine and as she told herself, very helpless. It was what she actually felt. Because she was so desperately in love with Harry it was impossible to think of not doing exactly what he wanted and what he asked of her.

"Perhaps he will get bored with me if I just sit humbly at his feet?" she told herself.

Then she laughed because she knew however much she tried they would be stimulating each other with new ideas. It would be impossible not to argue with Harry just for the fun of being defeated by him.

When she went downstairs to dinner, she saw he was wearing his best evening clothes. No man could have looked more handsome or more attractive.

He was waiting for her in the Drawing Room.

She ran towards him because it was impossible to walk slowly.

"You look lovely, my darling," he said, "just as I wanted you to look on our Wedding Day."

He said the words very softly, but she knew they meant as much to him as they did to her.

When dinner was announced they went in together. It was impossible afterwards for Teresa to know what she ate.

She guessed because Harry was downstairs, every effort would have been made to provide him both with the dishes he liked, and also the wine that went with them.

All she could think of was how handsome he looked sitting at the top of the table. How wonderful it was that he wanted her to stay with him and that he really loved her!

When dinner was finished he said quietly, "It would

be a mistake to go upstairs and I want you to come with me to the Study."

She wondered why.

When they reached the room that was particularly his and which had been his father's before him, Harry went to the drawer.

He drew out first a diamond tiara and then a short tulle veil to wear beneath it. She knew it might have attracted someone's attention if she had worn a full bridal veil. Instead, this just covered her hair, so that when she put the tiara on top she saw how becoming it was.

"This is the tiara my mother wore," Harry said, "and I always hoped that it would look as lovely on my wife."

"Thank you for letting me wear it," Teresa said.

He looked at her for a long moment, but did not kiss her. Then he drew from the cupboard, a small bouquet of white flowers. He put it into her hand and offered her his arm.

They went from the study along a corridor which led to the Chapel at the end of the house. Teresa knew the Vicar would be waiting for them.

When they reached the door, she saw an elderly man with white hair standing in front of the altar. What she had not expected was that Harry would have made the Chapel look so beautiful. The candles were all lit, six on the altar and two huge ones on either side of it.

The altar itself was covered with white flowers. There were huge pots of lillies in the Chancel. As she moved up the aisle on Harry's arm, the Vicar smiled at them.

When they reached him he began the service. It was very simple and yet it had a sincerity that Teresa thought she would always remember.

When they knelt for the Blessing she was sure that God was blessing them. As he had done already in letting them find each other.

Their love was the same love that had kept her father and mother blissfully happy for so many years.

When the service was over, the Vicar knelt down in front of the altar. Harry raised Teresa to her feet and kissed her very gently. It was, she knew, a kiss of dedication.

They went up the stairs together in silence. Then to her surprise Harry took her to a different room to the one in which she had been sleeping since she came to the Hall. This was a room which was next to the State Bedroom.

She guessed it had been occupied by his mother and every Countess before her. She realised that the room must have been closed up after she died.

On Harry's instructions it had been opened today.

The curtains were drawn back and the room seemed a mystical place where there was nothing but love. There were also, Teresa saw, white flowers everywhere as there had been in the Chapel.

She knew this told her that now she was in the same shrine in Harry's heart in which he worshipped his mother.

He did not have to explain that no other woman had ever meant this to him.

Because it was what Teresa had longed for she felt as if he had taken the stars from the sky and hung them round her neck.

The scent from the white lillies and the other flowers filled the air. As Harry shut the door, Teresa realised there was no maid to help her undress. Harry wished to wait on her.

He drew her close to him, kissing her gently but not passionately. The solemnity and the beauty of their wedding was still with them.

Then very gently, he took the tiara from her head and put it down on the dressing table, and removed the small veil. She felt his hands taking the pins from her hair so that it fell over her shoulders.

Finally he undid her gown and it fell to the ground. It was then his lips were on hers.

As he held her close and still closer against him, she felt the ecstasy and wonder of his kisses.

Harry carried her to bed and laid her down softly on the pillows. She felt she must have stepped into a dream because everything around her was so beautiful.

The stars and the soft silver light of the moon seemed a part of them both.

Then Harry joined her.

As he took her into his arms he said quietly, "I love you."

"And I love . . you with . . all my . . heart," Teresa answered, "but please . . darling, I am . . afraid."

"Of me?" Harry asked.

"No . . of course not, but I am . . afraid you will find me . . boring after all . . the beautiful women who have . . loved you before and I . . know so very . . little about . . love."

"Do you think I want you to know anything about it except from me?" Harry asked fiercely.

He kissed her eyes, her cheeks, her lips and then her neck. It gave her sensations she had never before known. It was so wonderful she could never have imagined it, and yet now it was real.

This was Love – this was Heaven on Earth.

Then, when Harry made her his, she felt as if they flew into the sky and touched the stars.

The moon which had been out of reach was in her arms and they were both very near to God.

"I love you . . I love you . .!"

The words seemed to be whispered on the moonlight.

"My precious, my darling, how can you do this to me?" Harry asked, "I love you as I never thought it possible to love anyone."

"I . . worship . . you," Teresa murmured.

He saw the expression on her face and knew she spoke the truth. She had surrendered herself completely and absolutely to him. He thought again that she was everything he had ever wanted in his wife.

At the same time, he knew her brain would inspire him to do great deeds. They would make the world a better place because they would both seek perfection.

He was silent, and Teresa whispered, "D . . Do you . . still . . love me?"

"I have no words to tell you how much," Harry said quietly. "You are like the lilies I had put in this room because, my precious, they are a symbol of you – untouched, innocent, and mine – completely and absolutely mine!"

As his lips sought hers Teresa could feel them igniting little flickering flames within her.

"Love me . . Harry . . please . . go on loving me," she begged. "I want your love . . I cannot live without it."

"As I could not live without you!" Harry answered.

She felt as if the flickering flames within her were leaping higher. They were joining with the fire which she knew was burning in Harry.

"I want you, I want you," he said, "give me yourself because you are mine – mine, my Darling."

"I am . . yours," Teresa answered, "yours . . completely. Oh! Harry . . love me. I want to . . love you as you . . want to be . . loved."

It was difficult to say the words because the ecstasy within her was part of the moonlight.

She knew that Harry was feeling the same.

They were closer than they had ever been, not only with their bodies but with their minds and their souls. They were alone with the stars above them and the moonlight was taking them into a special Heaven of their own.

Harry held her closer. Their love, he knew, would

triumph over every difficulty that lay ahead. The fire that consumed them both leapt higher.

"I love you . . I love . .!"

The words seemed to be murmured all around them and repeated in their hearts.

They were one, now and for all eternity.